MOJAVE MUD CAVES

Robert Essig

PROLOGUE

Brandy Freedman walked the quiet, desolate streets of Needles, California under the illumination of a nearly full moon. Up ahead a solitary red light blinked leading travelers to the bridge over the Colorado River, away from a sweltering land of broken dreams and crumbling facades toward the bright lights of Laughlin. Only the few bars were occupied at this time of night, and even those were sparse with locals who forever drowned away the oncoming heatstroke a hard day's work threatened over a seemingly endless string of 100 plus degree days and nights. But it's a dry heat. That's what the locals always said, like some kind of sad respite for a sadder existence.

On this night Brandy found herself disgusted and angry with a guy she thought she could actually trust, a man she gave her heart. Though she had given her body to plenty of boys in her formidable years and beyond, she held her heart close. It took a lot more than a romp in the hay to have a glimpse into the emotional depths of Brandy Freedman. She let Walt in, and now she felt foolish. She would be damned if she was going to be one of those women who live in an abusive relationship and make excuses for not leaving the bastard. She'd seen the type on *COPS*. They would call the police because their boyfriend got drunk and roughed them up, and then suddenly they were crying and insisting that he didn't mean it. No, officer, don't take him to jail. I don't want to press charges. Brandy wasn't mean and cruel, she understood that these women were trapped; she just didn't want to ever be caught in such a trap.

Besides, she'd seen that movie before. It infuriated her that another man could lure her into his greasy, overbearing clutches. How could she be so stupid?

Brandy walked past the flashing red light, buildings the color of desert sand to her left and right with faded signs advertising gasoline, medical marijuana, and jerky—beef, chicken, venison, and more!—a likely stop for folks taking advantage of the pot shop for the high rather than the medicinal treatment. She heard a car approaching and thought it might be Walt, the son of a bitch. She'd jumped out of his ice cream truck not twenty minutes ago in the parking lot of an abandoned gas station. It would take more than the comforting air conditioning to keep her from fleeing after what he did. She'd walk over screaming hot coals before going back to that asshole.

The car turned out to be a truck. It made a left at the flashing red light, heading over the bridge and into Arizona. Laughlin? Kingman? Anywhere but here. Brandy had thought about leaving. Living in a shithole town under the oppression of California law and crappy minimum wage jobs when Arizona was so close and the living was more affordable was almost as bad as going back to a sweet-talking abusive boyfriend.

The strange thing about living in the desert is that you really did become used to the oppressive heat. Air conditioning was key to survival, but Brandy could walk down to the corner store and back and hardly break a sweat, partly due to how dry the air was, but also how much her body chemistry had become adjusted to her environment. She was born and bred in Needles, somewhat of a fixture in town, and not for good reason. Her reputation preceded her. In a town as small as Needles everyone knew everyone, or at least knew *about* everyone from gabby gossipers and word of mouth. It wasn't uncommon for certain fanatical religious members of Needles to whisper "Slut" under their breath in passing.

Brandy turned nervously at a sound in the quiet night. The street was just as empty and sad as it had been when she jumped out of Walt's car. He'd honked his horn and cursed her and then pleaded with her. "I love you!" he'd said, and she'd kept on walking. Eventually "I love you" turned into "FUCK YOU, BITCH!" and he'd peeled out. If anyone heard and split their blinds long enough to make out Brandy's face and the tail end of Walt's ice cream truck, they had probably sighed and returned to their nightly television programs, figuring the town slut was at it again.

Nights like this Brandy wanted to be away from Needles more than ever, but further than Laughlin or Fort Mojave. She would come into contact with far too many locals. Everyone drove into those towns for groceries or to eat out. Even in Laughlin there was a good chance she would be recognized. Also, her parents lived in Needles. They divorced when she was four, her father hitting the road in a big rig, popping back into town whenever he was passing through, but not enough for Brandy to form the bond she would have liked to have with the man. Her mother slept around a lot. Growing up there were a lot of men in her life; none of them father figure material. Some tried getting fresh, and that's when Brandy learned how to defend herself. She kicked some asshole square in the balls and brought him to tears. He tried to cop a feel, but she wasn't going down like that. Let a perve do something like that and they'll come back again and again. Mother took the prick's side and Brandy left. She was only fourteen when it happened, and she had nowhere to go being that her father was blowing diesel on some great American highway. She considered fourteen to twenty-three the dark years. Now, at thirty-one, Brandy was over the shameful life she once lived, but the cruel people of a failing town would never let her forget.

Another sound. Brandy turned, certain someone (Walt?) was sneaking up on her.

Nothing.

She continued forward, toward the street where she lived in a singlewide mobile home with an old air conditioner that desperately struggled to keep the energy inefficient tin can at a cool eighty-five, when she heard the sound again, only this time it was so close she felt something breeze by her in a gust of warm air. She turned and no one was there. When she turned back, hands grabbed from behind. Brandy screamed and a hand clamped over her mouth. She bit, but her assailant wasn't deterred. After mere seconds of squirming, fearing who it might be and what they wanted with her, she felt a sharp pain in her back like an epidural.

She said something like, "Walt—!" and was out cold.

Chapter 1

The red Dodge Ram tore down highway 95 like desert driving was a competition. Considering the boat trailing behind the Hemi, it was amazing and frightening how bold Matt was when passing semi trucks and slowpoke drivers on two-lane blacktop. Matt and his friends were young enough to retain some of that youthful energy and lack of recognizing one's mortality as a fragile thing.

"Jesus-fuck!" Matt said, flashing a toothy grin. "Another caravan of sheeple trailing behind a puttering big rig. What's up with that? How the hell can so many people stand going so. Fucking. Slow?"

Sammy, Matt's best friend since they were monstrous little heathens riding bikes and taunting little girls, rode shotgun. "What's the record?" He swiveled to face Nikki, Shawna, and Ollie, all sitting on the bench seat in the extended crew cab.

Nikki said, "Four, I think." She raised her eyebrows in disinterest.

"Yeah," said Ollie. He had his arm around Shawna. They were the type of couple who thrived off public displays of affection, driving the rest of the truck crazy with kisses and the occasional baby talk. "We passed a semi and some cars an hour ago."

Sammy looked ahead at the tail of cars behind a silver eighteen-wheeler. "There's no way you can do that. Too many cars."

Matt grinned, cocked his sunglasses. "Oh yeah?"

With a friendship as deep as that between Sammy and Matt, Sammy knew what he was getting into after such a comment. Matt was the kind of guy who never stepped down from a challenge, whether offered or implied. He was the all around baddass who felt like he always had something to prove, and prove it he would, regardless of the consequences, which tended to get him into trouble from time to time. And the people who associated with him. He'd been kicked out of bars, ballparks, restaurants, banned from entire malls, and arrested a few times for outrageous pranks the likes of which would cause the maniacs behind the *Jackass* movies to cringe. Thing about Matt was that he could talk himself out of even the most sticky situation, which was the only reason his rap sheet didn't have its own filing cabinet. His family thought that PTSD after his stint in the military was to blame, but Matt had always been a wild one. He just seemed to get crazier with age. He lived his twenties like the challenge was to become incarcerated or killed before thirty.

As soon as the solid double yellow line turned into a single broken line indicating that they were safe to pass (not that Matt always abided that particular rule of the road), he pulled the truck to the left to get a good view of any oncoming traffic. His grin deepened as the train of cars he was to speed past came into view. The road was clear as far as he could see. Behind the semi truck were at least six vehicles, one of them a motorhome.

Matt's grin stretched across his face like there were hooks buried in the corners of his mouth with invisible fishing lines being yanked in opposite directions. This was a grin Sammy knew well. This was the grin Matt had when they first smoked weed, drank a beer, egged the principal's house, smashed car windows with garbage cans when they first got driver's licenses. It was an intoxicating smile with enough influence to cause a holy man to kiss the devil's ass.

"Buckle up, ladies and gentlemen," Matt said. "We're going to see what this hemi can do!"

The truck swerved into the opposite lane. Ollie and Shawna looked back as if fearing the boat trailer would become unhinged and cause a wreck in their wake. Shocked awe turned into smiles as Matt pushed his foot down on the pedal. The truck didn't lag a bit, just plowed forward with a jump from the RPM dial and a steady rise in miles per hour. They passed two cars. Matt gritted his teeth, muscles clenched. Hands gripped "oh shit" handles. Shawna clutched Ollie tighter. A third car and then a truck. The hemi threatened a hundred miles per hour, a speed that was frowned upon with or without a trailer. The truck ate dust and soon the motorhome, which was the last vehicle before the eighteen-wheeler.

"Sammy!" Matt said, pointing across the cab toward the passenger window, "moon these motherfuckers! They're the ones causing the backup."

Sammy hesitated, as if what was being asked of him took a moment to register in his mind, and why not? It had been at least five years since they'd driven around the many communities of San Diego County smashing mailboxes and mooning people. It was sophomoric, childish even, so Sammy, finding himself caught in the moment and raging with adrenaline, unbuckled, twisted himself around, and pulled down his shorts, pushing his ass cheeks up against the window, his balls hanging like a hairy cyst. Though Sammy was of Indian descent, his butt cheeks were pale in comparison to his dark skin tone. As they sailed by the motorhome, Matt tapped the horn. The truck erupted into laughter at the wide-eyed shock of the retirement-case sitting behind the wheel of the Weekend Warrior.

And then Matt screamed, "Oh fuck!"

Sammy scrambled to straighten himself out; expletives were slung like confetti. Up ahead, coming straight for them, was another eighteen-wheeler, sun gleaming off the polished chrome, black smoke piping from the huge exhaust pipes that protruded from either side of the cab like cylindrical steel ears. From this frightening vantage the front of the big rig resembled a menacing face, the grill a massive set of teeth ready to chew wrong way drivers and leave the wreckage on the sandy sides of the road.

Matt pushed the pedal to the floor. The engine picked up and the truck lurched forward. Without regard for the trailer, Matt yanked the truck back into the right-hand lane in front of the eighteen-wheeler just seconds before being creamed. The driver laid on his horn to which Matt laughed as he struggled to keep the Dodge from fishtailing as the boat trailer swung back and forth. The truck's rear tires screeched. Matt regained control and left the caravan in a blast of desert sand.

"You're crazy, Matt!" Nikki said without the slightest remnant of adrenaline-fueled glee she possessed only sixty seconds ago. She was pissed. "You're a fucking asshole, you know that. You could have killed us."

"Coulda, woulda, didn't," Matt said, laughing off Nikki's concern. She punched him in the arm. "Oh come on!" Matt smirked into the rearview mirror. "Live a little, huh. Don't tell me you weren't enjoying that before we almost slammed into that Mac truck."

"New rule," Sammy said. He was pale, shaken up. "No more passing unless it's, like, three cars max, 'kay?"

"Ah whatever, man. We're almost there anyway."

"Almost there?" Shawna said, eyes of confusion looking in

the rearview mirror from the back seat, but unable to see if Matt was returning her questioning looks due to his shades.

"Oh, I didn't tell you? We're going on a little excursion before we get to Lake Havasu." Matt's jaw dropped in mock surprise. "Ollie didn't tell you?"

Shawna glared at Ollie. He said, "Come on, Matt, I didn't know about this. What are you talking about, man?"

"Bullshit," Sammy said. "We talked about it at the Renegade that other night."

Shawna elbowed Ollie in the ribs. "You went to the Renegade?"

"Uh oh," said Matt, "someone's in trouble."

"Babe, I told you we went to the bar."

"I don't remember that?"

Nikki said, "So, what, was this something the boys decided without the girls?"

"Naw," said Matt, "just something we chatted about. My idea really. Ever heard of the Mojave Mud Caves?"

Nikki wrinkled her nose. "Mud caves?"

"Yeah, mud caves. In the mountains."

"We're in the desert. Where's the mud come from? And what's a mud cave?"

"There are hot springs all over the desert. What's a mud cave?" Matt put both hands up and shrugged. "Fuck if I know, but I heard they're really cool, and—" Matt squinted. "I think this is our road."

Matt slowed the truck as he took the unmarked exit that brought them to a dirt road that ran perpendicular to the highway 95, stretching either direction into shivering heat waves. The truck headed north toward the mountains.

"So where did you hear about these mud caves?" Nikki asked with a hint of concern.

Matt shifted in his seat. "There are all kinds of secrets out in the desert. There's supposed to be this secret little pool of water in a covered concrete tub with little solar panels that keeps the water cool."

"What's the point?" Shawna said, wrinkling her brow.

"Dunno." Matt shrugged. "Just some shit some really smart people did for fun I guess. I heard of the mud caves on the Internet. They're supposed to be in the wall of these mountains. There's a crevice that leads to an area in the middle of the mountains that you can't see from the desert. That's where they're at."

Shawna sighed. "So we're going to *hike* in this heat? Are you crazy?"

"I did the research. How do you think I found this place? It's not much of a hike, and supposedly the mud caves are in the side of the mountain. It should be cool inside."

"Oh great. You have us going into caves now. Awesome. You know what's in caves? Bats. When I was a little girl my family went on a trip and saw the Carlsbad Caverns. You go deep into these caves and get to this big room or whatever. Then the tour guide turns off the damn lights. I screamed so loud." Shawna shivered at the thought. "I'm not going inside. No way."

"Oh come on, don't be a grouch. It's not like we're going to camp out here or something. It'll be fun to look around."

"You realize it's over a hundred degrees out there, right? That's why we're going to the lake, to cool off and have fun."

"Let's not stay here too long," Ollie said. "I'm not exactly looking forward to exploring mountains in hundred degree weather either."

Matt pulled the truck to a stop at the base of the mountain. "Alright kids, grab your water bottles and walking sticks, this is where our search for the mud caves begins."

When they opened the doors the heat attacked them like an invisible blanket of molten lava. "Oh god," Sammy said. "I think I'll just wait here in the air conditioned truck."

"Don't be a pussy," Matt said as he pulled a cooler from

the bed of the truck that was hidden beneath a tarp. "I loaded this thing up with water and ice. We're gonna need it."

Nikki looked worried as she stared up at the rocky mountain. "I don't like this, Matt. Seriously. People go hiking at Three Sisters and Green Valley Falls back home in ninety-degree weather and have to be rescued due to dehydration and exhaustion. Do you really think this is a good idea?"

"Christ, people, when did you all turn into a group of limp-wrist pussies. Jeez, if we're burning out we'll leave. We're not idiots. That's what all the water's for. C'mon. Right around the corner here should be the crevice. Might even be shady."

Sammy smirked. "So what's that, a hundred in the shade, one-ten in the sun?"

"Something like that," Ollie said.

Matt took the lead without even looking back, and his friends followed, sipping water and already looking miserable. The sand beneath their shoes and flip-flops was firm enough so that they didn't struggle to walk. What little wind blew felt like an oven with a fan inside. Lizards danced by standing on kitty-corner feet and switching when the sand became too hot for even a cold-blooded reptile.

Ollie and Shawna took up the rear, walking far enough away from the others to talk privately.

"Matt's such an ass," she said, voice just above a whisper. "Why's he gotta be like that?"

"That's just Matt. He's had a bit of a complex since we were kids. I always figured it was better to be on his side than to have him against you."

"So you guys really went to the bar? When did this happen. Why didn't you say something?"

Ollie paused. He wasn't a great liar, couldn't think quick enough to talk bullshit and own it. It was his hesitation that told Shawna he was about to make something up, or come up with a plausible reason for his actions, not that going to the bar was the worst thing ever. Shawna had a tendency toward jealousy, and though Ollie had been told by his friends that he was pretty much pussy-whipped and should "be a man," he loved Shawna. His grandfather once told him that when people love one another they will overlook the small things, deal with the embarrassing things, and cherish the wonderful things about the one they love. Shawna's jealousy was a small thing, as far as Ollie was concerned, but he still felt awkward about things she disapproved of, such as going to the bar with friends. It wasn't so much that he went to the bar with the boys (she was cool with that if he told her ahead of time), but that he hadn't told her. She would be worried that there was a reason he hadn't told her.

"I just forgot. We were having beers over at Matt's and then we headed to the bar to talk about the trip."

"So you knew about this little detour we're on?"

"Matt mentioned it, but—"

"Here's the crevice," said Matt. "Keep your eyes out for sidewinders." The glee in his voice indicated the pleasure he got dragging his friends on such a seemingly mundane and exhausting adventure.

Shawna stopped at the giant crack that seemed to split the mountain in half. Ollie held back with her after the others followed Matt down what looked like an almost labyrinthine trail with huge walls of granite reaching for the sky at either side. It was shaded, but that was little respite from the sweltering heat.

"Look," said Shawna, "I really don't want to do this. It's stupid."

"I know, I know. I'm not big on desert hikes myself. We all want to get to the lake. I'm sure Matt'll want to turn back soon enough. He wants to go to Lake Havasu more than any of us. I'm kind of surprised he actually brought us here."

"What's with you guys, doing whatever Matt says like

he's some kind of messiah?" Shawna rolled her eyes. "The guy's a dick. I'm sorry, but it's true. He's a fucking asshole."

Ollie gave her a knowing grin. "You're not the first to say that. I kind of always liked having the guy on my side though."

Shawna wiped her brow and adjusted her sunglasses. "He isn't on *your* side, he's pushing you and Sammy around for his own amusement. Sammy doesn't seem to mind, but I can tell that it gets to you."

"Matt and Sammy have been best friends since before I even met the big ol' meathead." Ollie shrugged and tilted his head. "Matt's not so bad. He's like beer. An acquired taste."

Shawna tossed her empty water bottle. "I need another water."

"I'll lead the way. Not like we have keys to the truck anyway. We're kind of stuck out here."

"That's a comforting thought."

Together they slipped into the ages-worn crack that split the mountain. The sides of the massive fissure were lined with minerals that gave a glimpse into the age of the mountain like stripes of filling in a cake. The shade felt nice on their hot skin. Both Ollie and Shawna had their eyes on the ground scanning rocks and little dark hollows.

Ollie said, "Good thing is they've already gone through. If there were any snakes they're probably frightened off."

"I hope they didn't take some kind of turn."

"Just remember," Ollie's voice deepened like the announcer for a horror movie trailer, "the hills have eyes."

Shawna slapped his arm. "Knock it off, Oliver."

Ollie groaned. He hated when people addressed him as Oliver. That wasn't even his name. His parents were real hip skater types back in the eighties. He figured he was lucky his name wasn't kickflip or something. Shawna only called him Oliver when she was trying to get a rouse out of him. It used to really get his goat, but now he pretty much groaned it off.

"What happened to Nikki?" Ollie said. "She barely knows Matt and Sammy."

"Nikki doesn't need to know anyone very well to play along, especially boys."

"What are you trying to say, she's a skank?"

"You know Nikki. We weren't friends for years because she stole two of my boyfriends in junior high. Oh, I hated her for that. She was such a slut in high school it was sickening. I guess part of it was just jealousy. She seemed to get any guy she wanted. I don't know if she was fucking them or what, but that gives a girl a reputation. But we reconnected in college."

"Oh yeah, you told me about that. She changed, right?"

"I guess. You tell me."

"What do you mean? You asking if she's made a pass at me?"

"Deep down I still have a little resentment. I kind of figured a weekend at Lake Havasu aught to tell me what kind of person Nikki really is. Doesn't surprise me she took off with two guys she hardly knows."

"Shawna!" Nikki's voice echoed through the winding rock walls. "Shawwwwna!"

Nikki didn't sound particularly distressed, but both Shawna and Ollie picked up their pace. After a couple of sharp curves in the rock the mountain opened up into a tiny valley where the ground widened and desert shrubs grew in abundance. The sand became softer here, and up ahead at the other end of the plane was a huge wall of the mountain so unusual in appearance that both Ollie and Shawna stopped and stared, awe-struck.

"We found it!" Matt's voice was small coming from across the little valley. His excitement was palpable.

"I thought we lost you guys," Nikki said.

"Holy shit," Ollie said. "What the hell *is* this?"

The mountain ahead rose into the sky like some primitive

building. On its face were huge holes with what looked like mounds of dried mud freckling the massive façade. There was no wind, no animal sounds, nothing but desert quiet and this strange sight before them.

Matt's voice carried through the valley, dwarfed by the spectacle before Ollie and Shawna. "I present you with . . . THE MOJAVE MUD CAVES!"

CHAPTER 2

A few hours earlier

Big Vic stood at the kitchen window with a cup of coffee reflecting semi-retirement and watching people milling about on the street, about as lively as they ever were in the middle of summer in Needles. A sip of coffee, sun, already glinting off of everything, a constant reminder that he was in for months of almost constant seclusion in the house or a movie theater, a trip to Laughlin or maybe some fishing at the river. Maybe not so much fishing. Brandy wasn't an outdoors type of girl and Big Vic wanted to spend more time with his daughter this summer. He hadn't always been there when she was young. As a result, he felt partially responsible for her fall from grace. Now that he had enough money stowed away to take some time away from the open road and the never-ending long haul, he wanted to reconnect. Not being there for Brandy during her formidable years was one of Vic's great regrets.

For the past five years they had the summers together, as well as a week here and there between jobs. Vic owned his big rig, which afforded him the ability to pick and choose his jobs. Hauling goods across the country was his specialty (paid nicely, too), but he would haul specialty items for private clients if the price was right. He sent money home for Brandy to buy groceries and necessities for the house. Vic had always thought his children should be out of the house by twenty-five. He had that independent all-American ideal of getting a career and starting a family. The Freedmans had never been college-bound and Big Vic just didn't see that changing. When Brandy was little he struggled to make ends meet, and then Denise left him.

Such ponderings always threatened to stun the beginnings of a great day. Way Big Vic saw it, any day in retirement was a good day, and though he wasn't technically retired, that's how he liked to refer to his summers. It wasn't a vacation. Wasn't time off. It was semi-retirement. It was lazing around with coffee, maybe a beer at night, good food in an air-conditioned paradise.

One look around the house assured Vic he wasn't exactly living in a paradise, but it was what he had. It was his domain and he wasn't fool enough not to be proud of what he worked for. Yes, he could use a house cleaner (if only he could depend on Brandy to pull her weight), but it wasn't so bad. And he wasn't a pig. The furnishings were old and mismatched and the drapes were the same drab eighties throwbacks that were in the house when he bought it. The idea of remodeling or renovation was lost on Vic.

After refreshing his coffee Big Vic went into the living room and took a seat in his favorite recliner, so shaped to his frame that it was uncomfortable for others to sit in. That or it was so old and worn that it should be replaced. Vic liked it, and that's all that mattered. The house was small, just 900 square feet with a Jack and Jill bathroom that always became a point of contention between he and his daughter. When she was readying herself to go out (like last night) and Vic had to take a shit, things got hairy. She would lock both doors and he would have to hold it until she was good and ready to get out of there. No amount of pleading and yelling at her to open the door would get that stubborn girl to let the poor man relieve himself.

But, Vic reflected, she's on a better path now. If she would just stop seeing that guy . . .

Vic didn't hear Brandy come in last night. He hated when she stayed out late, but he wasn't going to treat her like a kid. She would always be his little girl, but she was thirty-one now and he was making up for lost time. Perhaps today they could . . .

Vic set his coffee cup on the little table beside his favorite chair. There was a corner of the coffee table that was ominously absent of Brandy's purse. It could be in her room, he supposed, but she always put her purse on the end of the coffee table, on the side of the couch she sat as regularly as Big Vic sat in his recliner. It was her spot. And her purse was always on that corner of the coffee table. She never brought it into her room. The rooms were so small that she spent most of her time in the living room when she was home. Since she moved in with Vic five years ago they became close and enjoyed one another's company with a mutual respect for the barriers between their friendship and their father-daughter relationship.

She'd gone out with that Walt punk last night. He wasn't a punk, per se, but Big Vic called any young man with rings in his face and sleeves of tattoos a punk. He didn't like the way Walt sneered; could tell at a glance that he was one of those anti-establishment anti-authoritarian liberal pukes he tended not to get along with. Politically Vic was a middle of the road guy who leaned to the right, though he contended that both sides of the aisle were equally clueless and flawed. People like Walt were on another level. Anarchist, socialist, communist. Some kind of -ist.

Vic glanced over his shoulder at the door to Brandy's

room. Though he tried not to let it show, Vic worried about her. If she knew how much he worried it would bring her down, cause her to reflect on her past. It took a lot for her to forget that past, and there were reminders everywhere in a town as small as Needles. Her past lingered in the abandoned buildings, the railroad tracks, the glaring eyes of the locals, and her own mind. She'd been on a good stretch, but this Walt character made Vic nervous. He wasn't worried about the guy in a defensive sort of way. Big Vic didn't garner such a moniker for nothing. What worried him was that Walt would bring his little girl back to the dark side. Vic wouldn't be there to hold her hand, and after the summer he would be on the road again for a month straight.

Vic wouldn't be concerned about her missing purse had it not been for Walt.

It was ten-thirty. Brandy wasn't known to be an early riser, so that wasn't unusual, but Vic had a bad feeling stirring in his guts. Something wasn't right.

He went into the Jack and Jill bath. It looked the way it had when he used the bathroom after waking up. Or at least he thought it looked the same. If there was some little differ-ence, he didn't notice it. The toilet seat was up. Now that Vic thought about it, hadn't the toilet seat been up when he used the bathroom this morning? Surely had Brandy come home last night she would have used the can at some point, and she always left the seat down the way he always left it up (another point of contention).

Vic put his ear to the door from the bathroom to Brandy's room. He couldn't hear anything. He didn't want to try the doorknob. Didn't want to creep her out. Anyway, it was too early to be concerned enough to attempt entering her room.

But Vic was concerned nonetheless.

He returned to the living room. His coffee was forgotten about, maybe resting on the bathroom counter. Once the feeling of something bad settled, it changed the appearance of even the brightest day. Suddenly smiles looked mean and frowns depressing.

Big Vic stood at the front window, watching cars roll by. The street he and Brandy lived on was a popular route taken by locals. He was familiar with most of the cars and trucks. Some passed by like clockwork, particularly on weekdays, going to work, the supermarket, the post office. Ronnie Blanchard walked by everyday at nine in the morning to get his daily bottle of Coke. Vic never understood why he didn't just buy a case at a Bullhead City market and save a few bucks. Maybe it was the routine, something to do before the heat really ramped up. Marci Black walked her dog every morning around six. Gary Houston jogged by.

Vic spotted a familiar vehicle, one that made rounds every day when the school got out. The ice cream man. He also just so happened to be Walt Miller, Brandy's boyfriend.

Vic watched the ice cream truck roll down the street wondering if Brandy was in there. Had she spent the night with Walt? Vic couldn't be upset with her. She was an adult and could do whatever she wanted to, but in his mind she was still his little girl. Vic once heard that long-term addicts who get help and finally stop using will mentally go back to the age they were when they started using, that the years in-between were lost to the substances they abused. Vic often thought that the years he was away while Brandy was growing up were similarly lost, and that she would be his little girl for a long time to come.

The ice cream truck pulled up along the curb in front of the mailbox. Vic turned and went into the kitchen, occupying himself with the task of searching out his lost cup of coffee. He didn't want to see Brandy get out of the truck, didn't want to see her shame. In the past five years there had been a few times she stayed out all night, being dropped off or walking home early in the morning. She called it the Walk of Shame, but Vic didn't ask her to elaborate on just what that meant.

He could pretty much figure it out. Right now he'd rather not be standing at the window like some worried parent who had stayed up late in wait for their mischievous teenager.

Instead of the familiar sound of the deadbolt turning and the door opening, there was a knock.

Big Vic wrinkled his brow. Did Brandy forget her key?

He went to the front door and opened it, ready to embrace his little girl if she needed it. He couldn't say that he would be sorry if Walt had kicked her to the curb. She didn't deserve it, but Walt didn't deserve her. On the other side of the door was Walt with his trademark scowl, eyes droopy like he woke up with a bowl of weed rather than Wheaties. If there was one feature Big Vic despised as much as facial jewelry and tats, it was a damned soul patch, that little triangle of hair between the lip and chin. Walt had one of those. A soul patch was a sure sign of cockiness and arrogance as far as Vic was concerned. It was a stamp that might as well read: douche bag.

Face completely stoic and void of emotion, Vic said, "Where's Brandy?" He had completely abandoned the possibility that she was asleep in her room.

"I, uh, was coming here to make sure she got home all right last night. She left pretty mad with me. I fu— I messed up pretty bad." Walt had his hands planted in his pants pockets. He sort of twisted his arms nervously like a child with ADHD. He couldn't stand in one place and have a conversation, but then again Big Vic had that affect on people. He was built like a fucking bouncer, and right now he wasn't happy.

Vic's face deepened into a scowl. "I thought she was with you."

Walt's eyes widened from the lazy stoner normalcy that Vic was used to. "She didn't make it home last night?"

"Well . . ." Vic turned and looked at Brandy's door. Was she in there? "I don't know. I haven't seen her. Her purse isn't on the coffee table."

"You're kidding, right? She's here. She's gotta be. She was walking this direction when she left."

"Left? Where were you?"

Walt found it difficult to make eye contact with Big Vic, also a part of Vic's intimidation, but also because he was hiding something. "We were in my car over at that old gas station. You know the one, by the jerky place and the pot shop."

Vic's eyes narrowed. "What were you doing by the pot shop?"

"Dude, the stores were all closed. We were just sitting in the car talking. We didn't want to hang at my pad with my roommates."

"So you just let her walk in the middle of the night?"

Walt moved around nervously and ran his fingers through a messy rat's nest of dreads on his head like some west coast surfer-dude. Another attribute Big Vic looked down upon. What the hell did Brandy see in this guy? He was dirty and kind of smelled like BO and stale cigarettes.

"Look," Walt said, "you know how Brandy is. She gets all upset with me and runs off, she doesn't want me coming after her. Doesn't work that way. Gotta give her space, man."

Vic nodded. He knew perfectly well what Walt meant. Brandy was a hardheaded girl. Always had been. That was why Vic had to wait for the restroom when she was prettying herself up. You had to choose your battles with Brandy, because she could hold a grudge with the best of them.

Concern came over Walt's face. It was a look Vic could relate to, a look he was kind of surprised to see. "So she's not here?"

Vic let a deep breath out through his nose. His voice lowered in an almost sympathetic way. "I don't know. I'll knock, tell her you're here to apologize." Vic's eyes locked on Walt and his brows deepened enough to amp up the natural intimidation his body language screamed. "That's what you were going to do, right? Apologize?"

Walt nodded. "Yeah, yeah." He swallowed hard. "That's the idea, man." He pushed a thick dread behind his ear. It was dark at the roots, but the end was bleached out and kind of looked like an old cat turd.

Vic nodded and turned, but he didn't invite Walt into the house, just left the front door open. Walt had been to the house before to pick Brandy up, but he had never been inside. Walt and Brandy's relationship was fairly secretive, which had always bothered Vic. But again, he wasn't one to pry.

At Brandy's door, Vic knocked lightly, hoping he would rouse her from some deep sleep. She would be angry with him for waking her, but it would be worth it just to know she was there. He would gladly kick Walt to the curb and go on with his day, beginning with a fresh cup of coffee and an even fresher perspective.

There was no answer.

Vic knocked louder. Still no answer. He called her name, looked back at Walt who stood patiently at the front door. Well, maybe not patiently. He was kind of pacing back and forth like a comical image of a father-to-be in a maternity ward waiting room. Vic turned the door handle and gently pushed open Brandy's door. She wasn't there. Her bed was made up, completely undisturbed.

CHAPTER 3

G ATHERED TOGETHER AT THE BASE OF THE MOUNTAIN WITH THE odd-looking mud caves, Matt and his friends mentally prepared for something most of them hadn't left San Diego hours ago intending to involve themselves with.

Shawna and Ollie stood together, though it was too hot to snuggle like they normally would have. She gave him a few kisses after he reassured her that he would speak up if Matt took things too far. His words seemed to soften the edge she had developed.

Though Nikki had only met Matt and Sammy this morning when they embarked on this trip, she could tell that they had a strong connection that years of tight friendship would account for. They were easy to talk to, which was nice since Shawna had a tendency to proclaim her love with public displays of affection that made Nikki want to puke. The boys didn't seem too outwardly attracted to Nikki, at least not in the creepy way some guys were toward women in close proximity, sneaking glances at her cleavage and whatnot, and that was a good thing, because she was going to have to hang with them at least until they got to the lake. Matt was super excited about the lake and Sammy was on the shy side, only opening up in the presence of his more boisterous and outgoing best buddy. Nikki figured he would clam up were he and Matt to become separated.

"What do you think is in there?" Nikki said. "Mountain lions?"

Matt shook his head. "No way. Too hot for mountain lions. They live in the type of mountains with trees 'n' shit. I don't know what lives in these caves, but I think we should go inside one and have a look."

Matt didn't catch Nikki's sarcasm. He obviously thought she was a dolt or perhaps liked to throw around his Mr. Know-it-all swagger. She figured a bit of both, considering his macho attitude. He wasn't so bad, though. Nikki had known much worse men in her life. Besides, she liked a man with confidence. It appeared that Matt had more confidence than both Sammy and Ollie combined. The problem with a guy like Matt was that Nikki herself had a good deal of confidence, and that always had the possibility of leading to head butting. Nikki had seen guys like Matt back when she was a kid and her father would bring her to the mountains just outside of San Diego for target practice. His Navy buddies were a lot like Matt. Sometimes you just had to humor them.

Above them the wall of the mountain was sporadically dotted with large mounds of dried mud, each with a hole at the center, as if someone had managed to bring wet mud onto the rocky mountainside and built weird little caverns.

"Where's the mud come from?" Sammy said. "Reminds me of, like, a mud wasp's nest, or one of those huge subterranean termite nests in Africa."

Matt laughed. "You're fuckin' crazy, Sammy. Subterranean termites? Really? Mr. Encyclopedia Britannica over here. Who knows what this is. Let's check it out." He looked at his cell phone. "We've got an hour or so. I don't want to get to Lake Havasu too late, know what I mean?"

Everyone murmured agreements. No one seemed all that

enthusiastic about exploring the caves, but no one was going to disagree with Matt. Not yet at least. Shawna looked at Ollie like he was supposed to do something, but he either didn't get the hint or ignored her.

Most of the cave-like openings were too high up the mountain for easy access, but there was one low enough to reach with a little amateur rock climbing.

"That's the one," Matt said. "Everyone wore their hiking shoes, right? Flip flops need not apply."

"I'm not going up there," Shawna said.

"It ain't shit. Looks harder than it is, and really it's not that high up. Here, I'll go first."

Matt walked around the rocks that looked as if maybe they had been excavated from the hole where the mud had been packed into the mountain. Could have been the result of a dynamite blast, or some bizarre natural phenomenon that caused the base of this particular mountain wall to be scattered with boulders of all shapes and sizes.

"Watch for snakes," Ollie said.

Matt scanned the rocks from the best route of access. "You bring your anti-venom?"

"Sorry, dude. Must have left it with my safari hat."

"Then we all need to keep our eyes out for rattlers. We're, what, fifty miles away from Needles, and I don't think they have a hospital."

Matt found the path of least resistance and made an example by climbing to the mud encrusted cave without too much trouble. Being fairly competitive by nature, everyone followed him up. Ollie helped Shawna, though she didn't really need it. He liked to show her that he cared, that he was concerned about her. He felt mildly responsible for this unusual excursion and knew she was putting on her best veneer despite how much she despised Matt and his selfish ideas of fun.

At the mouth of the cave they stared into its dim depths.

Sammy scratched the dried mud, rubbing the earthen sand between his fingers.

"Any one bring a flashlight?" Ollie said.

Matt pulled a small LED flashlight out of his pocket and clicked the button. The beam shot out in a tiny circle that grew quite large with a twist of the flashlight's head. Everyone stared into the cave as Matt slowly traced the contours with the glowing beam. Inside the cave was completely covered in the strange dried mud that crept out like excess foam used to plug a hole after a home repair. The sides were smooth and broke off in several directions in multiple tunnels, presumably connecting to the other holes in the mountain.

"Whoa," Sammy said as he followed the light's beam. "I didn't know what to expect, but this is crazy. What the hell is this?"

Shawna shook her head wearily. "Something did this."

Matt smirked. "No shit, Sherlock."

"But what?" Nikki said. "Like, a bear or something?"

"No bears, sweetheart. Just like mountain lions they stick to the forest. There aren't any large predatory animals out here. Mountain goats, rattlers, shit like that. This is a phenomena."

Ollie looked into Shawna's eyes, registering her fear. He said, "Naw, something did this."

Matt slung his backpack off his shoulders and onto the ground. He opened it and retrieved flashlights. "Here." He had one for everybody.

Nikki eyed Matt with suspicion. "You came prepared."

"Had to. I knew you'd all just pussy out on me, and I didn't come all this way just to look into the caves." Matt zipped his backpack and slung it back over his shoulder before stepping just inside the mud-crusted lip of the cave. He directed the beam of his flashlight under his chin like someone telling scary stories around a campfire. "Right this way folks. The tour starts here."

Matt ventured into the cave.

Shawna shook her head and let out an exasperated sigh. "We're not really going in there, are we?"

Sammy shrugged and followed Matt inside. Nikki said, "It is kind of cool, in a spooky sort of way."

Ollie gave Shawna his best sympathetic look, which was more pathetic than sympathy. "Look, Matt doesn't want to be here all day or anything. He's got his heart set on drunk girls in bikinis. Let's just humor him for a minute. What's it gonna hurt?"

Shawna rolled her eyes. She had a way of rolling them that made her eyelids flutter. She did it on purpose to let whomever she was directing her ire towards know for sure that she was indeed upset. Ollie had seen those eyes flutter and roll enough to know that she was at her wits end, but he really didn't want to start any problems. They all had to spend another hour or so in the truck together, and Matt was, for better or worse, the navigator. Without him they were screwed.

Ollie put his hand on Shawna's shoulder. "Baby, when we get to the lake we don't have to hang with them. We can find a nice place and have some alone time."

"What about Nikki? She came along because I invited her. I'm not going to ditch her."

"What about her? I'd say she's fitting in better than you are." Ollie immediately regretted saying that. He could see that he'd hurt her.

Shawna's eyes deepened "You're a piece of work, you know that, Ollie." Shawna put her hands up in a dismissive gesture and walked into the cave, flashlight leading the way.

"Where are you going?"

Shawna turned and gave him a "duh" gesture. "I'm fitting in!"

She stormed off. Ollie stood there with the sun beating down on the back of his neck, thinking about what had just happened and the complications this incident would have on the rest of the trip. Shawna was high maintenance, Ollie didn't need anyone to tell him that, but running off into a cavern of mud caves alone wasn't a bright idea. He was beginning to wonder if this trip was such a good idea. It was supposed to be fun, and maybe it would have been if Matt didn't decide to bring them into the middle of the desert to see some fucking caves.

Flashlight in hand, Ollie went in after Shawna.

The cave was dark, but not completely blacked out. There were light sources—probably the other cave opening up and down the side of the mountain—that created a dim aura too faint for the human eye to see by. Ollie directed the flashlight in all directions, surprised at the vacancy of the cave. Where did everybody go? Where was Shawna? She didn't even want to go inside and now she seemed to have taken off with reckless abandon.

The cave itself was strangely circular, like a huge drainage pipe made of smoothed mud that was put through a massive kiln and dried as hard as the Death Valley floor. The substance was darker than desert sand, as if from another source, a deeper, more organic source. However the cave was created, the dirt had a more mineral substance than that of long-bleached desert sand. Venturing further within, Ollie came to several offshoots of the cave, all tubular. Some went straight up and others jetted off to the left and right. Because the ground was solid, there were no telltale footprints to follow, so Ollie decided to holler, "Shawna!" His voice echoed through the dried mud tubes. "Matt! Nikki! Sammy!"

After calling into several of the cavernous tubes, Ollie began to feel like he was being pranked. Had Shawna's outburst been some kind of rouse to separate him from the gang? No. Couldn't be. If she could act as pissed as she was, she had a lucrative career in Hollywood. Her frustrations were real, and probably short-lived, for Shawna loved Ollie deeply enough for them to get over the small stuff with relative ease. Ollie just hoped that this trip didn't get out of hand.

"Fuck," Ollie muttered. He walked along the various openings. "Hey, guys, seriously, stop fucking around. I know you're in one of these chambers."

Shawna was right, he thought, this is a waste of time and a bad idea. What if they get lost in there? What if they came face to face with whatever made these tunnels? Ollie had been an avid fan of horror and science fiction since he was a kid. Matt called him a nerd sometimes, but that didn't bother Ollie. Matt was always tearing people down. Ollie was used to it. He'd seen movies like *The Descent* and *The Hills Have Eyes* enough to know how bad a situation like this could become. He didn't actually think people made stupid decisions like splitting up in some unknown cave in the middle of the Mojave Desert. If there was a staircase and some axe-wielding madman was chasing them, it was now clear to Ollie that they would surely go right up those stairs.

After further consideration, Ollie decided that he could go into each circular cavern just enough to see where they went. He would turn back before getting lost. Surely he would find someone, and when he did he would insist that they find everyone and get the hell out of there. Matt could be a pretentious and domineering prick, but even a born follower like Ollie had his limits. Problem was, Ollie tended to go off like a bomb when he was pushed to his limits. Came as a result of bottling up his emotions and keeping quiet when he should express himself. Shawna hadn't seen that side of him, because he was careful not to blow up at her, but there had been times when something went terribly wrong and an unfortunate person, say a merchant or clerk, got an earful. He was all bark and no bite, though. Fighting had never been a viable solution in Ollie's mind, even when he was pushed to his breaking point.

Ollie ticked off each new tunnel, "Eeenie, meenie, miney, moe, catch an asshole by the toe." He stopped on a middle tunnel, but decided for the one on the far right, that way he could keep track of which ones he'd explored.

The tunnel was round like it had been bored with some kind of specialized drill. These could be mines for all Ollie knew, but something about the slender caverns caused him to deny that notion. Going forward the tunnel rose steadily, but not so quickly that he couldn't keep his footing. The flashlight beam illuminated solid, dried mud smoothed out like a concrete pipe. He couldn't see too far ahead due to the slope and twists and turns the tunnels made. The sharp turns were unsettling, not knowing what was around the corner and fearing the worst imaginable things. Blind, pale creatures with venomous fangs, zombified miners with infrared sight, giant menacing vampire bats with fangs like ice picks.

Eventually Ollie came to a split. Deciding that it would be foolish to choose one side or the other, too easy to make a mistake in retracing his steps and become lost in what may be a labyrinthine maze of tunnels, he hollered, "Shawwwww-naaaa! Maaaat!"

Either they weren't down there, they were too deep to hear, or the joke was going on way too damn long. Ollie turned back.

The caverns were cooler than outside in the desert, but still warm. Certain chambers created wind tunnels that pulled in hot air from some unseen opening that created a vacuum, while other tunnels were still and desolate. The quiet was the worst. No sounds of footsteps, voices of Matt's sarcasm and Sammy's goofy laughter. Also, there wasn't evidence of animals. No bat dung, snakeskins, bones or fur. No burrows that a coyote would use for a den or holes for smaller varmints.

After the third tunnel Ollie decided to go back outside to see if everyone else had regrouped. A bad feeling gnawed at his guts. He would have heard something. How do you not hear Matt's obnoxious voice? You could identify where he was in a supermarket if you closed your eyes and listened. Ollie wasn't one to scare easily, but this whole situation had him on edge. If they weren't out there, he didn't know what he was going to do.

As he reached the opening that cast a perfect circle of light through smoothed edges, he heard something familiar that caused him a great deal of relief. Ollie emerged from the cave and couldn't help but smile as the heat assaulted him, the sun's devil sunrays violating his skin. He shook his head like it was all some elaborate joke, even chuckled, though none of the group could hear. They were down in the valley laughing and joking around.

"You guys got me!" Ollie said, perched on a large boulder before the cave opening.

"So the lovers emerge," Nikki said with a smile that, had Ollie not been devoted to Shawna, he could get used to.

"You guys finally done in there?" said Matt. "We gotta get on the road. I almost sent a fucking search party."

That's when Ollie's grin of blessed reassurance dropped. *You guys?*

He counted heads, frantic and hoping that he'd heard Matt wrong. One. Two. Three. That was it. Shawna wasn't hiding out there somewhere, not unless she was crouched behind a rock taking a piss. Yeah, maybe that's it, Ollie thought. She's just squatting behind a rock somewhere.

The three stood there looking up and though their faces were indistinct from the distance between them, Ollie could tell that something was wrong. They had that look you see in horror movies when someone sees something creeping up behind a friend, but doesn't want to alarm them. Ollie looked over his shoulder, fearing that something would indeed be there sneaking up on him. He saw nothing but the faint renderings of the vacant cave.

"Where's Shawna?" Matt said. His voice had a slight twinge of concern, which was a rarity for the chucklehead.

Ollie's mind scrambled. "She's not with you?"

All three heads swiveled in the negative.

"Oh fuck!" Ollie turned, flashlight at the ready. The three voices of his friends were in a panic. He couldn't distinguish what they were saying, but the general sense of concern and shock was heavy. Ollie exited the cave again just in time to see his friends run across the valley. He followed their trajectory and saw, across the way, someone coming out of another opening that was low to the ground. He couldn't make out the figure but it was stumbling, collapsing on itself and struggling to navigate the steep grade of rock that led down from the cave to the floor of the valley. Ollie climbed down the rocks like an expert and rushed to meet up with his friends.

By the time he made it to the woman who had emerged form the caves, he could see that she was as pale as a catfish's underbelly and smudged with dirt and grime. What little clothes she had on were torn and stained with something that looked like bad underarm sweat stains.

Ollie finally made it to his friends, who had surrounded the woman. Matt turned, his face grave (something Ollie couldn't remember ever seeing), and he said, "It's not her."

CHAPTER 4

After discovering that his daughter hadn't made it home last night, Big Vic rushed to the front door, grabbed Walt by the shirt collar, and pulled him into the house. "What the hell happened to her?"

Walt quaked. His body erupted in full-blown trembles. Wasn't such a tough guy under the tattoos and piercings. "I didn't do nothing to her, man. Let go of me!"

Recognizing the fear in Walt's trembling body, Vic steadied himself and took a deep breath. He wasn't a bruiser anymore, hadn't been for a long time. On the road he would hang at certain trucker bars across the country, and you'd better know how to throw a punch, because some of those guys were tough as nails and had a hair trigger for violence. Vic should know. Hang around with that lot enough and a saint goes sinner in no time.

Big Vic let go of Walt, who then stepped backward without letting Vic out of his sight. "What's wrong with you, pops?"

"Pops? Who the fuck do you think I am, buddy? Your father?"

Walt shook his head and got all fidgety again. "I call all dads pops, man."

"Don't call me that. Seriously. Now look, what happened last night? Why did Brandy run off?"

Walt became even more uncomfortable. "She just got upset, that's all."

If Vic's eyes could deepen any further, they did just. "What did you do?"

Walt had a hard time looking Big Vic in the eyes. He sighed and opened his mouth as if to say something, but his words were caught in his throat. "Look, man, she gets like that, you know. She gets upset over stuff."

"Stop beating around the bush. You did something, didn't you?"

"I didn't touch her." Walt's eyes kept darting to the front door, to the windows.

"I don't know that for sure. I'm certainly not taking you on your word. Not until we find Brandy, and she better be safe or it's your ass."

"We?"

"Yeah, we. You're all I have to work with to find her. That girl's been through a lot in her life and she's finally straightening her shit out. Has been for several years now. I haven't always been there for her." Vic took a lungful of air and exhaled deeply, shaking his head, overcome by shame. "I promised myself I would always be there for her when she needed me. I'd drop everything to help her. I love that girl." Vic had a way of staring into someone's eyes that forced them to look, even a twitching bag of shit like Walt. "If you've done anything to her I will hurt you."

"Are you threatening me?" Walt became defensive rather quickly, like he had some hidden lawyer or something.

"Yep. We're going to retrace her steps as best we can."

"Fuck you. I've got my routes to make."

"No you don't."

Walt found something within, maybe frustration, maybe a sense of survival. He stepped forward and said, "Who the fuck do you think you are? You can't make me do shit!"

The veins in Big Vic's neck bulged. He lurched forward and gripped Walt's pencil neck, slamming the skinny little shit into the wall. He reared back his right hand in a fist that looked about as big as Walt's peanut head.

"Don't punch, man!" Walt pleaded. "Don't punch!" Tears welled in his eyes immediately.

"Remember this next time you think you're a tough guy. Maybe with the girls you are, but with me you're not. Got it."

Walt sniveled.

"GOT IT!"

Walt nodded as best he could with Vic's hand bracing his throat. "Yeah, got it."

Big Vic let go of Walt's neck. Walt rubbed his Adam's apple. "You're crazy, pop—dude."

"You might be dating my daughter, but you don't know me. And you don't know crazy like a father whose daughter is missing."

"Maybe she crashed out somewhere. Maybe she stopped at a friends house or something."

"She wouldn't do that. She's cut ties with a lot of the people she ran around with back in the day."

"Oh yeah?"

Vic squinted his blazing eyes. "There something you need to tell me?"

Walt shook his head. "Naw, man. It's just you might not know everything you think you know about Brandy, that's all."

"Do you care about her?"

This question seemed to catch Walt by surprise. "Well, yeah, I guess so."

Big Vic smirked and kind of snorted. "You guess so, huh? I don't know what she sees in you, and I don't mind saying it.

Come on. You're gonna show me where you were when she walked out on you, and if there's some friend of hers you know about, some place she may possibly have gone at that time of night, you better tell me. Until we find Brandy I'm holding you personally responsible."

Walt clicked his tongue. "Dude, really? I didn't do shit?"

Vic said, "Come on, let's go."

Vic drove his truck to the abandoned gas station where Walt and Brandy had their argument last night. It was hot out, but Vic insisted they huff it and retrace Brandy's steps. If there had been a struggle after she left Walt maybe she left something behind, a shoe, her purse, something. They found nothing.

Walt insisted that there really wasn't anywhere Brandy would have gone, no friend's house she could crash at. He had introduced her to several of his friends, but she was more comfortable when they spent time together, alone. Walt said that at first he thought Brandy was stuck up, but later realized that she had all kinds of deep ties with all kinds of people in town, and that she purposely tried to avoid confrontations.

Vic used a handkerchief to wipe sweat off his forehead. "We have to go the sheriff."

Walt went pale. "Whoa! What? You pulling my leg or something, pops?"

"Enough with the pops shit. Seriously, knock it off. Yes, the sheriff. The quicker we report her missing the quicker they start looking for her."

"She's an adult. Doesn't she have to be missing for like at least a day or two?"

"I'm not waiting that long."

Walt used the sleeve of his shirt to wipe his brow. "I'm sure she'll show up. She was mad, man. She needed some space."

"From you. I know my daughter. She would have come

home." Big Vic smirked. "What, you got something against the police?"

Walt became reserved. "Who likes the cops? They kill people."

"Oh jeez. Who are you gonna call when someone breaks into your house in the middle of the night?"

"Not the cops."

"Sure. Come on."

After an absurd amount of protestation and veiled threats, Walt got into Big Vic's truck. Walt insisted that they were wasting their time, that Brandy was holed up with friends somewhere, but if he had any idea of who her friends were he wasn't talking. Eventually Big Vic stopped listening to Walt, but the guy wouldn't shut up. He was like a wind up toy that never ran out of juice, like he had a promising career in a pink rabbit costume as the Energizer Bunny. Good thing Vic had patience. The bad thing was when he ran out of patience. And Walt was pushing it.

CHAPTER 5

MATT AND SAMMY HELPED THE PALE WOMAN TO AN AREA WHERE the mountain created shade, which brought the temperature from one-hundred-ten to one-hundred-four. Her body was cool, but warming quickly. Her mouth was crusted in vomit and she'd lost her bowels and bladder at some point. Her eyes rolled back, pupils struggling to focus.

"Are you all right?" Matt said.

"No, she's not all right," said Nikki. "What a stupid question." Nikki knelt down beside the woman and said, "How did you get here? Are you here with friends?"

The woman's eyes rolled to whites and her body went slack, head lolling.

"Grab her head!" Matt said.

Sammy recoiled. "Dude, she's got puke in her hair 'n' shit."

"Christ, dude, don't be a pussy." Matt grabbed the woman's head and, with the assistance of Nikki, repositioned the woman so that her head wouldn't smack against a rock. He put his hand over her heart. Sammy started to say something, but Matt shushed him. After breath-held seconds, Matt nodded. "She's alive. We gotta get her out of here."

"Wait, what?" Ollie said. He'd been watching his friends and the unknown girl between glances at the various cave openings. There were so many of them across the mountain. "What about Shawna? She's lost in there somewhere."

With Nikki acting as nurse, using a bottle of water and a bandana to wipe the girl's face clean, Matt stood and said, "Fuck! We just can't leave this chick out here. She's in serious trouble, man."

"Yeah, so is Shawna. We should be in there looking for her."

"Why the hell did she walk off anyway, huh? How stupid is that? You don't just walk through caves like this on your own. Everybody knows that."

"Oh knock it off, man. This isn't the time or place, okay. Shawna's in danger, and we've got to find her."

"He's right," Nikki said. She folded the wet bandana lengthwise and placed it over the unconscious woman's forehead.

Matt wiped sweat off his forehead. "So you two think we should just leave this girl here to die and go in there looking for Shawna? Dude, she's probably all right. Probably just looking for us."

Ollie shook his head. "Won't hurt to go in there and look for her too. You can stay out here with her if you want. That's fine. If you could climb up the mountain and get a signal on your phone and call the police, that's even better."

Matt grew impatient, but managing to keep his cool. "Or me and Sammy could drive her into Needles, get her the help she needs. We'll send cops out here. They could probably bring a dog to find Shawna if you guys don't find her by then."

"You're fucking kidding me, right? You're suggesting leaving us out here in the desert? You're gonna take the truck?"

"Look, man, no matter what someone's going to be left out here. It's fucked up, but I don't see a way around it."

"I do. Me and Nikki and Sammy go looking for Shawna. When we find her, all of us head out. All at once. It's the right thing to do."

Matt kicked a patch of sand in frustration. "The right thing to do is to take this girl into Needles where she can get help. I'll send cops. They'll do a hundred with their lights on or send a chopper or something. I'll drive as fast as I can. You guys keep all the water, maybe hole up in one of the caves until help arrives. That's all we can do."

"Bull shit!"

Matt took several stomping steps toward Ollie, face tightened up, eyes blazing. "Well that's what we're doing, whether you like it or not. I'll drop you right fucking here, prick. Just make a move."

"Okay, calm down," Nikki said, shocked at Matt's sudden outburst. "You guys are acting like a bunch of steroid meatheads. I'm sure we can figure something out."

"I did," Matt said. "C'mon, Sammy, let's crutch her out of here. You take one side, I'll take the other."

Ollie and Nikki watched in disbelief as Matt and Sammy gently lifted the woman the way one would a drunken partygoer. She was completely slack in their arms. Sammy, quiet through the bickering between Ollie and Matt, went along with what Matt said, as he had all his life like Matt was some kind of jocular guru. Had he stood with Ollie and Nikki perhaps there would have been a different result.

Ollie's mouth hung open in shock. "So you're really going. You're going to leave your friends behind?"

Matt grunted, shifting the woman into a more comfortable position. "She *needs* help, man. Don't worry, we'll call the police as soon as we get some bars. We're not walking out on you, we're taking care of business."

Ollie opened his mouth to protest, but nothing came out. He was silenced in utter disbelief. To Ollie, Nikki said, "Come on. Let's look for Shawna, but we have to stay together, okay?"

Ollie watched as Matt and Sammy struggled through the sand, the woman's feet dragging behind like rudders, leaving a pair of shallow troughs to mark their way. He nodded. "Yeah, sure, okay. Let's go."

They entered the caves through the same opening they had all entered initially. Once inside, they both called out for Shawna, but heard nothing more than their own voices echoing through the strange tubular tunnels. Not the type of echoes heard in a vast cavern that rang clear and crystalline, but more of a reverb effect that seemed to become absorbed in the crusty walls.

Ollie set the ice chest in the center of the cave. "Look, lets leave this here. If Shawna sees it maybe she'll stick around. I wish we had something to write a note on, tell her to stay here until we get back."

Nikki rubbed the floor with the tip of her shoe. "There's no sand in here. It's so weird. It's like compacted dirt."

Ollie nodded. "Yeah, there's something I don't like about these tunnels. I've been inside caves before, and they're nothing like this. Hey, so which direction did you guys go when you came in here?"

Examining the various tunnel offshoots like a woman standing before a line of suspects at the police station, she said, "Uh, I don't know. I think that one." She pointed to the middle tunnel. "But I can't be sure. I wasn't paying attention when we came in here. It was all fun and games, you know?"

Ollie nodded. "I looked through all of these others on the left. Let's start over here. Grab a water."

Each equipped with a bottle of water, Ollie and Nikki took no more than three steps before they heard a whooshing noise from one of the tunnels like a sudden, concentrated gust of air.

"What the fuck was that?" Nikki said.

"Dunno. A gust of wind?"

"No way. There's, like, no wind at all outside." Nikki cupped her hands around her mouth. "Shaaaaaawnaaaaa!"

They stood silent for a minute, eyes adjusting to the dark, but heard nothing.

"C'mon." Ollie gestured for them to move forward. "Let's start searching the tunnels. She's got to be here somewhere."

They took one of the center tunnels that had the kind of steep incline that puts great stress on calf muscles. The tunnel winded left and then right before leveling off a bit.

Nikki kept glancing at Ollie as if trying to figure out what he was thinking, or perhaps looking for a way to initiate a conversation. His face was shadowed heavily in the weak glow of their flashlights, stoic, concerned. "So what were you two fighting about?"

Ollie looked sidelong at Nikki. He could see genuine interest in her eyes, not just the interest girls have in juicy gossip, but genuine concern, as if by knowing the extent of their argument would somehow assist in them finding her best friend. "Things couples argue about."

"Vaguebooking a little? Seriously, what's up with you two? I know Shawna can get kind of possessive at times. Remember, I've known her since we were little girls. She's been known to run off like this. One time when we were teenagers we were with these boys at a park drinking forties of Mickey's. Her boyfriend at the time said something stupid that really set her off. I don't remember what he said. I don't remember it being particularly awful, but she lost it and walked." Nikki giggled in reminiscence. "I ran after her eventually. Found her three blocks away. She said she was going home, but was walking in the wrong direction." Nikki laughed nervously, a deliberate attempt at lightening the mood.

Ollie remained humorless. "It's not funny. Running off

somewhere back at home is one thing. Out here she could be in real danger."

Nikki shot Ollie a somewhat disdainful look. "I'm just letting you know that this is normal for her. Doesn't really shock me, although she picked one hell of a place to pull one of her stunts."

"She was pissed about coming here."

"To the lake?"

"No. Here. This place. The mud caves. She thought it was a stupid idea, and then she got all bent because I wasn't standing up to Matt."

Nikki smirked. "He is kind of a douchenozzle, isn't he?"

"Kind of?"

They continued walking, though at a slower pace. Strange, earthen odors lingered in the stale air. They called out Shawna's name every five minutes or so. Their voices ceased to echo, as if they were zeroing in on a dead end.

"We should turn back," Ollie said.

Nikki squinted, pointing ahead. "What's that?"

"Oh great. Just what I feared. The tunnel forks."

"Which way should we go?"

"I'm not so sure it's a good idea to take either way. Could get lost."

"But . . ."

"Let's just leave this bottle of water." Ollie took a swig from his bottle and then knelt down, placing it on the smoothed brown floor where the three tunnels met. He placed the bottle on its side, pointing the cap toward the tunnel they had come from. "That way it will serve as a sort of arrow, you know, just in case she comes by this way."

Nikki nodded. "Okay. We can take one of these tunnels then. As long as we don't take another branching tunnel, we can come back and use your arrow to figure out our way back."

Ollie stared at the bottle. Without a flashlight it would

have been easily missed. "You think that's a good idea? Would Shawna have gone this deep?"

Desperation settled in. Nikki bit her lip, as she did when she was nervous. "I don't know." She pulled her phone from her back pocket out of habit or like it was some kind of beacon to lead their way. She grumbled and put the phone away, which was enough to tell Ollie that there were no bars. Of course not. It was hard enough getting a signal in the deep desert, and more so in the middle of a mountain.

"Which way?" said Ollie. "Left or right?"

Nikki shrugged. She looked like she was on the verge of tears. Her attempt to lighten the mood with an anecdote had been a way of dealing with her fear. Something as ominous as the tunnel splitting created a whole new canvas for fear to run wild.

Deciding on the left-hand tunnel, Ollie took the lead. Nikki followed close behind.

"I'm getting scared," she said. "Where is she? Why can't we find her?"

Ollie's flashlight beam danced ahead of them. "For all we know these tunnels criss-cross all throughout the mountain."

"Don't say that."

"I can't believe Matt left us."

"What a prick. I know that woman needed help, but how could he do that? What if he doesn't come back? What if he doesn't send help?"

"He'll send help. He's kind of a dick, but he wouldn't do that. He did four years in the Marines. Afghanistan. I think they have a motto about not leaving anyone behind."

"Then why did he leave us behind?"

Ollie grunted. "I don't know. In his mind he can save everyone, I guess. Serving your country doesn't give anyone a pass from being an asshole. Matt was always a pretty abrasive dude, but when he came back he was different. I don't know, maybe PTSD. He doesn't talk about his service much. I don't think it did for him what he hoped it would."

The tunnels were much cooler than the desert, though still warm. Both of them were sweating, but Nikki was absolutely dripping. She was distraught and nervous, almost shaking. "I don't like this. I'm starting to panic."

"Don't panic. We can get back to the opening real easy, okay? Maybe we should go back." Ollie stopped and positioned his flashlight beam to see Nikki's face, but made sure not to blind her. Her eyes were wide and glassy.

Nikki blinked several times. She averted her face from the light, preferring to look at the ground. "Why would Shawna go so deep into the tunnels? That's not like her."

"What do you mean? You said you had to walk three blocks to find her that one time she took off."

"Yeah, but that was back at home, not in the middle of the desert. If she didn't want to do this, why would she get herself lost? It just doesn't make sense."

"Well," said Ollie, shining his flashlight ahead, illuminating a dead end.

The air left Nikki's lungs, leaving her deflated. They stared at the dead end for a moment before Ollie said, "Hey, look at that."

"What?" A tremble wavered Nikki's voice.

"Strange how the dead end isn't covered in this weird layer of dried mud. See," he shone the flashlight closer, illuminating chunks of ragged granite that glinted in the beam of light. "Rock. That's what the inside of a mountain should look like."

Nikki touched the rock, running her fingers along the jagged edges, testing one to see if she could pull a chunk free, but it was solid. There were chunks of rock that had fallen on the smoothed-out floor. This was a work in progress, a tunnel to be dug and lined with expertly smoothed mud that dried like adobe, and yet there was no evidence that human hands had done this. No signs that humans had ever entered the caves.

Suddenly Nikki perked up. Ollie took notice and tuned his ears in. "What is it?"

"I hear that noise again. The whooshing noise, only it's getting louder."

Ollie perked up his ears. "Yeah, I hear it too."

The disturbance sounded like wind through a turbine off in the distance, growing and growing until it more resembled some kind of vehicle speeding toward them at high velocity. There was no rumble of a motor, just the sound of something rushing through the tunnels.

"Jesus!" Nikki said. "What's that?"

All Ollie could do was shake his head as the sound intensified. The whoosh turned into an incredible buzzing like a swarm of bees that somehow synched their wings. Down the tunnel from where they had come a form appeared, caught in Ollie's flashlight beam. Nikki put hands over her ears and knelt down, eyes clamped shut, tears breeching the lids. She screamed as the thing approached, but her shrieks were drowned out by the approaching hum that caused her brains to vibrate, her ears to tingle like they were planted against a subwoofer.

The thing came upon them with such speed that they were both shocked, unable to respond, and then it attacked. The buzzing stopped and before them, caught in trembling flashlight beams, was something with huge wings and at least a half a dozen arms that appeared human in form, yet were charcoal in color and shining as if polished. The thing moved quickly, grabbing Nikki. She shrieked and squirmed in a sudden panic. "Get it off me!" Her flashlight fell to the ground, casting the beast in writhing shadows.

The shock of seeing this abomination caused Ollie a moment of hesitation. The thing was recognizable in its monstrous state, but so absurd that Ollie could only stare as it attacked Nikki before he snapped out of the trance and grabbed a loose rock from the ground. He held the flashlight firmly in one hand, the rock in the other. Ollie raised the rock above his head and belted out a war cry as he attacked the thing that was using its many arms to grab at Nikki.

The beast cried out a piercing screech, its slender insect-like body writhing. The many human-like hands gripped Nikki tighter, and then the black, bulbous abdomen curled, pointing a dagger-like stinger at Nikki. Ollie hit the thing with the rock, but its body was covered in exoskeleton armor and the rock bounced off, sending a reverberation through the bones in Ollie's arm. He managed to keep his grip on the rock, but hesitated before laying out another blow.

The massive bug injected Nikki in one quick jab, holding the stinger in her flesh as it depressed poison into her body. She screamed and writhed within the many hands that held her body tight. The wings fluttered faster than the eye could follow. The thing lifted itself, hovering just below the rounded ceiling, and shot through the tunnel like a projectile, leaving Ollie with the fading buzz of its wings.

Ollie dropped the rock and then crumbled to his knees, watching the empty tunnel and unable to comprehend what he had just been through. His body trembled, causing jerky, flickering light that cast bizarre shadows through the still beam of Nikki's still flashlight on the cave floor.

Now both Nikki and Shawna were gone.

And Ollie was all alone in the middle of the mountain.

CHAPTER 6

"I can't believe I'm voluntarily walking in to the sheriff's station," Walt whined.

Big Vic smirked. "Better than being brought in cuffs, right?"

Big Vic had his hand on the door handle to the sheriff's station when he noticed Walt halt. "Look," Walt said, "I don't have anything to do with whatever happened to Brandy, I mean, you know, if something happened to her. I wouldn't be stupid enough to come here if I had something to do with her going missing, and I don't even think she's missing. I think she's—"

"Yeah, yeah, at a friend's house somewhere. You know as well as I do that she doesn't have a lot of friends in town. Not anymore."

"Maybe more than you know of, pops."

"Well, you're not talking and that's why we're here. Just come in and tell them what happened. That's all I'm asking. If I need you I'll find you. You realize that if she doesn't show up in a day or two that you're wrong, right?"

"About what?"

"Everything. I know my daughter. I've spent a lot of time

with her since she straightened out, and I've always hated you. I figured you were bad for her, and now something happens." Vic put his hands up. "I can't always be there to protect her. She's a grown woman. But I can look out for her. Now come on, let's get in out of this heat and talk to the upstanding sheriffs of Needles, California. I'm sure they would like to hear what you have to say."

The sheriff's station smelled of coffee, an aroma that was no doubt permeated in the walls and plastic plants that wouldn't stand a chance outside real or otherwise. A woman sat at the front desk busying herself with papers, a phone cradled to her ear. Behind her were a series of desks, some empty, others with officers filling out paperwork, sipping coffee, looking bored. On the opposite side of the room were more desks behind which were seated a pair of dispatchers, one of them jotting down notes as he spoke with a resident in distress.

Vic and Walt approached the front desk and patiently waited for the receptionist to finish with her phone call. She took her time after hanging up the phone, not looking up, shuffling papers as if she could will Big Vic and Walt away, or like she hadn't even seen them, which was unlikely. Finally she looked up, all heavy eyes and sass, and it was very clear that she had seen them come in and was waiting until she was damn well ready to greet them with her cold stare.

"How may I help you," the woman said. Her hair was too dark for her face, a dye job to hide the gray, but it couldn't hide the wrinkles and deep frown lines from the bad attitude she so effortlessly exuded.

"I would like to report a missing person," Vic said.

"Who would you like to report missing?"

"My daughter."

She paused a beat, her eyes looking up at Vic with something like pity. "You're sure she didn't run away?"

Big Vic was taken aback. "She's thirty-one years old."

"I see. How long has she been missing?"

"She didn't come home last night."

The receptionist's eyes had a way of scolding, especially the way she tilted her head down to look above her reading glasses. "She's not missing, sir, not yet. It has to be at least forty-eight hours before you can file a missing persons report."

"I told you," said Walt, staring at Vic like an irritated child.

The receptionist shifted her gaze toward Walt by rolling her eyes in his direction. "And who are you?"

Walt looked at her with great suspicion, unable to answer such a simple question.

"He's her boyfriend, I guess," said Vic. "Not that I approve."

"But you don't think she's missing," said the receptionist, her gaze never leaving Walt's twitchy face that was now shellacked in sweat.

Walt hiked up his lip like he was trying to compete with the receptionist's attitude. "Naw. She's probably at a friend's house."

"He was the last one to see her," Vic said, regaining the receptionist's attention.

She looked from one man to the other, sizing them up, before subtly changing the composure of her unrelenting stare, offering just a glimmer of compassion toward Big Vic. "You have reason to believe this man is somehow responsible for your daughter's disappearance?"

"Oh come on," Walt said. "Sounds like your ganging up on me."

Big Vic relaxed a little, as if someone punched a valve stem on his body to release a little air. "I just wanted Walt here to tell an officer what happened last night."

"Well, we technically can't do anything until she has been missing for over forty-eight hours, especially concerning adults. People up and walk away sometimes. This close to Laughlin people sometimes find themselves in the casinos and lose their sense of time."

"Brandy doesn't gamble," Vic said. "I know her. Something's wrong. She would have come home last night."

The receptionist raised her eyebrows. "Brandy . . . Freedman?"

Big Vic sighed. He could hear in the receptionist's voice that she knew of Brandy Freedman. Everybody did. The old Brandy, that is. He nodded. "That's her."

Now the receptionist lowered her head and tipped her reading glasses down further on the bridge of her nose. "Look, I'm not one for gossip, so I don't care either way what kind of reputation your daughter has, but I really can't do anything until tomorrow, not unless you have reason to believe she was abducted or harmed in any way. Do you?"

Vic took a deep breath, held it for a second or two, as if contemplating some kind of half-assed lie to speed things along, and then said, "No. She didn't come home last night, that's all."

"Right." The phone rang. The receptionist pulled it from the cradle and held her hand over the mouthpiece. "Hopefully I won't see you tomorrow." She then answered the call, completely averting her attention.

"Look, I told you, pops," Walt said.

"Cut it out with the pops shit. Seriously."

"I'm outta here, man. You can't hold me, you know. I'm an innocent man, and Brandy isn't missing."

"What's with you anyway? You aren't concerned in the slightest."

"That's because she isn't missing. Why don't you get that?"

"Why are you so sure?"

Walt just shrugged and smirked and was about to leave the sheriff's station when the doors burst open and two men entered, dragging a filthy, pale woman. "She needs help!" one of them said. "Quick!"

The receptionist stood, phone still planted to her ear. Her eyes filled the reading glasses. She looked back, alerting the deputies fiddling around their desks, both of whom rushed to the lobby for assistance.

"We found her in the desert," said one guy. "The mud caves. She's weak, maybe dying."

One deputy used his walkie-talkie to call for an ambulance.

Big Vic craned his head to see the woman, breath held, and then he saw her face, turned to Walt and said, "Not her."

Walt moved in closer. One of the cops glared up at him. "Stand back, please."

Walt stopped, but continued to stare at the woman. "That's Delanie Gruber."

CHAPTER 7

NIKKI WENT COMPLETELY NUMB WHEN THE STINGER INJECTED her. She could feel the poison enter her bloodstream and travel through her body, systematically paralyzing her, and yet her mind was sharp, cognizant, like someone put to sleep for surgery who wakes up but cannot alert the surgeon. It was a horrible feeling, the helplessness, something Nikki secretly feared all her life. Her panicked mind screamed, but her mouth didn't so much as open to release the surge of terror quelled within.

She used to suffer from claustrophobia. Once, when she was a child, her parents bought a new refrigerator and let her play with the box it came in. Nikki would crawl into the large cardboard box and close the ends, just to see how much she could handle before using her hands or feet to open the box for fresh air and light. She'd overcome the claustrophobia years later when she would experience panic attacks in the tight confines of the back seat of her mother's two-door sedan. She used mind power, something she had never actually studied, but deeply believed in. She would close her eyes and enter a sort of meditative state, only then could she banish the rising vibes of claustrophobia-induced panic and relax in the back of the car. Now, in the clutches of several humanoid arms and hands, that horrible feeling of claustrophobia swelled in her mind only this time she couldn't close her eyes and enter that meditative state.

Nikki was completely helpless, and terrifyingly cognizant of the fact.

The thing gripped her tight and navigated through the circular tunnels at roller coaster speeds. Nikki feared a cataclysmic collision, but the beast knew its way, expertly maneuvering the turns, the ups and downs, like a greased ball bearing.

After tense minutes of breakneck traveling, the thing slowed before shooting into a huge cave that reminded Nikki of something familiar that she couldn't place in a mind that was catching up from the blurring ride. She was nauseous, but unable to sooth herself, to so much as rub her belly. She could breathe and that was about it. Snot ran from her nose and dribbled over her lips. She couldn't even move her tongue. Her chest beat rapidly from the excitement. As Nikki's eyes regained the ability to focus, took in her surroundings, she realized that something was terribly wrong. The buzzing she'd heard before being attacked was more intense. Massive creatures roamed the cave in rigid movements like something out of a science fiction novel. And then she saw the unusual wall, the hexed patterns and wriggling things. Her stomach lurched and vomit cascaded from her mouth and down her lax, unresponsive body.

Ollie felt helpless within the depths of the mountain. By the time he made it back to the water bottle he and Nikki had left behind as a guide marker, it was facing the curved wall of the tunnel rather than the direction leading the way out. He had a good idea of which way they had come from, but wasn't sure which direction he wanted to go. Now he was responsible for both Nikki *and* Shawna.

Being alone in the dark tunnels was unnerving. The silence was so blank it screamed at him like an old television on a static channel. His mind hissed and screeched and distorted thoughts became inflated and absurd, sort of reminding him of the first time he smoked weed. The stuff had gone right to his head. He and a friend had snuck into an abandoned house to smoke the small amount of pot they had proffered from some loser at school. A neighbor must have seen them and went in looking around. Ollie and his friend hid in a closet under the stairs in the dark with nothing but their twisted minds run amok, the wild new high turning their thoughts into an amalgamation of weird distortions that threatened a madcap mixture of laughter and screams. The darkness of these tunnels, when Ollie looked away from the beam of his flashlight, caused him to feel like he had that day in the closet. If the light were to go out, he would probably scream and run. Even thinking about the fullness of the dark without a light caused a great deal of panic, a hidden claustrophobia he wasn't aware existed within.

Ollie passed the water bottle without replacing it in the direction he thought led to the tunnel that led to the ice chest. It would serve as a landmark for he or anyone else who would be searching. Hopefully the police. It wasn't very encouraging to put so much faith into Matt. The stuff about him being a Marine was more to calm Nikki than anything. After Matt did his four years he disavowed the Marines entirely. Ollie had heard the once a Marine, always a Marine mantra and hoped Matt felt that way, even if only subconsciously.

Ollie hadn't gotten a good look at the thing that gathered up Nikki. It must have been some kind of animal, but the sounds it made were unlike anything he had ever heard. It sounded like a giant bee, something from one of those old atom age B-films where radiation turns bugs into huge menacing monsters. Ollie had seen a few of those movies, most notably the one about giant ants called THEM! Cheesy as hell, but fun to watch with like-minded friends who enjoy the whole Mystery Science Theater aesthetic. Whatever it was that took Nikki, it had flown through the tunnel with expert precision, and that terrified Ollie.

Maybe it was a giant bat?

As Ollie walked and the darkness crept up on him, he was sure that what had taken Nikki wasn't a giant bat. He was sure it wasn't a bird. He was sure that he didn't know what the hell it was, and he was becoming more and more terrified that it would come back for him. Ollie wasn't a hero, never considered himself the bravest of men, but here he was walking through eerie tunnels inside a desert mountain looking for his girlfriend and her best friend like he was going to find them and save them from some monstrous thing that could fly, that knew these tunnels inside and out. That could probably see in the darkness.

Ollie walked on, cursing Matt and his dumb-ass ideas. He convinced himself that Matt would bring help, but would it be too little too late? They could all be at the lake right now, drinking brew, listening to music, and watching all the craziness ensue. Hundreds of coeds converged in one place with a tidal wave of booze and pounds of weed, not to mention the sea of eye-candy. Tequila shots had a way of making bikini tops fall off.

He periodically switched hands with the flashlight and the rock to prevent cramping. It was kind of a large rock, but the only thing he had for protection. If confronted again he would bash the beast first and ask no questions later.

With the darkness and the solitary beam of light, Ollie soon became acquainted with his fears, rationalizing them the way he had when he was a child. He had a way of soothing himself when he was afraid of something, be it a horror movie or snakes or spiders or whatever. He had told himself that spiders were good because they were a part of nature's cycle. Without spiders there would be an abundance of flies. Without snakes there would be an abundance of mice and rats.

Without flying cave monsters there would be . . .

Consciousness came and went in flashes of dim light, intense sawmill buzzing, and the sensation of being dragged along the cave floor.

Nikki was placed atop some kind of soft, squishy pile that smelled of minerals and sweat. Her mind swam like she'd had too much to drink. Stomach muscles involuntarily clenched with overwhelming nausea.

They were bees, she was sure of it. Giant, mutated bees, and yet the thing that attacked her in the tunnels grabbed her with too many human-like hands. The fingers had felt like little metallic digits that pushed into her muscle meat hard enough to separate the sinew into points of screaming, fiery pain.

Nikki blinked her eyes over and over, but they were leaking uncontrollably, blurring her vision like looking at the world through layers of plastic wrap. If only she could move, just will her arm to move so she could wipe her eyes and see what was going on around her, for she could tell that there was more light in this cave than there had been in the tunnels.

She was completely paralyzed. Helpless.

But Nikki *did* find that she could close her eyes, which was preferable to watching a dim cave of bee creatures through thick sap. With her eyes closed she could focus on that meditative state she used so many years ago to allow herself to ride in an elevator or sit in the back of her mother's cramped sedan. She called it mind power. It wasn't anything like The

Force Luke Skywalker used in *Star Wars*, but she was convinced that tapping into some deep mental recesses allowed her to overcome claustrophobia. She had never used the mind power to attempt anything other than a quick cure for her fear of confined spaces.

Nikki became somewhat calmed, though uncomfortable on the strange pile, particularly the areas where her muscles had been damaged by the creature's hands. She focused her mind on one act. All she wanted to do was move her arm, and once she did that, she would focus on moving her hand and wiping the gunk from her eyes so she could see what was going on. Focus on her arm. Nothing but her arm.

Around her the buzzing was consistent and shifting from one side of the cavern to the other. A whoosh of warm air breathed upon her when one of the humming beasts zipped by, all of which created fissures in her concentration. Her arm wasn't going anywhere.

Nikki lost focus and mentally slumped. Then a familiar feeling hit her, a terrible feeling. The cave's warmth seemed to grip her, to press against her flesh like a sauna. Fear reared its ugly head. Nikki opened her eyes but the goop covering them was just as good as looking into an abyss, which turned the fear to panic. Nikki couldn't move, but her breathing escalated into hyperventilation. Her heartbeat accelerated.

Oh fuck, oh fuck, oh fuck . . .

Claustrophobia was cured by eliminating herself from the situation in which caused the panic attack. Exit the car. Stop at the next floor to get out of the elevator. Close her eyes and tap into the mind power, her safe place.

Nikki closed her eyes. Her shifty, uncontrollable breathing was much like a child after a particularly bad crying fit, but she had to dig deep, had to lose the world around her and slip into that peaceful meditative state.

Oh fuck . . .

Her breathing calmed.

Oh fuck . . .

Then her breathing leveled. For a moment Nikki couldn't even hear the buzzing of the flying abominations in the cave. Her racing heart slowed and took on a normal pace.

Nikki knew for sure that she still had the ability to use mind control. She just had to focus.

The constant buzzing was worse than a persistent, swooping and dive-bombing gnat, loud like white noise or the fuzz on an old TV with the volume cranked. The kind of noise that didn't cradle ear canals, but forced entry. It was hard to think of anything with that buzz. Hard to think about how badly this situation could go. Hard to think about how nice it would be in the sun on the lake. Hard to think about Shawna and what happened to her.

Hard to think about nothing.

Hard to gain focus.

But that's what Nikki did. She closed her eyes, took a deep breath, and exhaled slowly. Treating the buzzing like the soothing rush of a waterfall or a sound machine, Nikki thought about nothing at all. Didn't think about moving so much as a finger much less an arm or leg. Just her and the buzzing.

The sound intensified and then hit a steady rhythm like a comforting heartbeat. The hot air became tolerable. Nikki breathed evenly, ignoring everything that happened around her, all of the little noises that could easily distract her, the strange (human?) odors of what lay beneath her. The weird slurping noise to her left. The scratching sounds echoing on her right.

She flexed her fingers. Still not thinking. Wiggled her hand in a circular motion, as if trying to get circulation back. Then she raised her arm, gesturing toward her face like one does when doing a field sobriety test, only her hand, intending on wiping the gunk out of her eyes, missed the mark like a drunk and tapped her cheek. From there she wiped her face clean, rubbed her eyes, and opened them.

Had Nikki not already been in such a fragile state, had she not been almost completely numbed, she would have screamed.

Chapter 8

"So how do you know Delanie Gruber?" Ike Spooner said.

Walt fidgeted in his seat, much the way he did when Big Vic had given him the third degree. Ike Spooner (known on the force as Spoon Man—something he was tagged with in the academy when Soundgarden had a smash hit by the same name) had been on the force long enough to tell a bull-shitter, and he knew how to deal with one. And he knew Walt.

Walt swallowed hard. "She's a friend of a friend. I don't know her all that well. Just seen her around."

Ike Spooner nodded, his stoic clean-shaven face giving no hint at all as to which way this impromptu interrogation was going to go. No, Spoon Man assured Walt, you're not in trouble or anything. We just want to ask you a few questions. Walt knew better. Spooner would do anything to get him behind bars. Had been trying for years.

"When was the last time you saw her?"

"I don't know, man. Like I said, I don't really know her. Probably saw her at someone's house."

"But you know her name."

Walt shifted uneasily. "Yeah, so?"

"Just trying to find out what happened. How she ended up in the desert."

"Dude, I have no idea."

Spooner glanced at Big Vic, and then returned his dagger-eyes to Walt. "You dating his daughter, that right?"

"Yeah, sure."

"She missing?"

Walt tapped his foot to some unheard speed metal beat. "Look, I don't have to sit here right? I mean, you don't have a warrant or anything, and I didn't do anything."

Spoon Man didn't even flinch. No emotion. No hint as to what was going on in his brain. "You're right, Walt. Free to go. But let me tell you something." Spoon Man leaned in. "You don't answer my question, you don't look so helpful." He squinted his eyes. "You don't look so helpful and I start thinking you have something to hide."

Walt stood up, regarded both Vic and Spooner with contempt, and headed for the exit. Spooner called to him, "Don't go far. Might need you back for more questions. Don't make me go looking across state lines for you. Kind of makes a man look . . . guilty."

Walt stopped, hands against the push bar on the door. Just a quick pause as the officer's statement sunk in, what, to Walt, sounded like a presumption of guilt, and then he walked out.

"What do you think about that boy?" Spooner asked Vic.

Vic took a moment to articulate his thoughts rather than blurt out his gut response of 'I think he's a son of a bitch.' " I've seen his type on the road. Can't trust him far as you can throw him. I think he's got plenty to hide."

Spooner nodded. "Yeah, I kind of got that feeling too. Too defensive about knowing that girl. Thing is, we don't have anything against him, and I don't think there's a chance in Hades that he would have come here with you if some girl he left out in the desert might show up like that. 'Sides, did you see the look on his face when he saw her?"

"Naw, I was too shocked at the look of her."

Spooner nodded. "Well, that Walt boy looked just as shocked." Spooner shook his head, showing for the first time some kind of emotion as he took in a deep breath and exhaled coffee fumes through his nose. "Thing is, it wasn't guilt-like shock. He looked shocked just like you did. Shocked at the look of the woman, not at *who* she was. It took a few minutes for that to sink in, his recognition. Vic, I kind of believe the bastard."

"What about my daughter?"

Spooner allowed another glimpse of emotion to rear its head by way of a minute sympathetic cock of the head and shifting of his mouth that accentuated his frown lines. "Don't know what to tell you. It isn't fair, but the truth is she hasn't been missing all that long. She's her own woman, Vic. What you've told us, there are no signs of violence, nothing suspicious really. Nothing to go on." Spooner put his hand on Big Vic's shoulder. "But don't fret. We've made a report and I want you to follow up with us if you don't hear from her by tomorrow morning."

Vic nodded his head, something he felt like he'd been doing a lot of here at the sheriff's station. "I'll tell you this. I don't like Walt. I don't trust him."

There was a commotion as the front doors opened and a pair of EMTs entered the station. They knelt down around the pale girl who was propped in a chair and covered in a heavy blanket, immediately asking questions and preparing to take blood pressure.

Sheriff Spooner stood, which prompted Big Vic to do the same. Spoon Man offered his hand. "No offense, but I hope I don't see you tomorrow, Vic."

Big Vic shook his hand, nodded, and left the sheriff's office.

CHAPTER 9

THE WOMAN SLIPPED IN AND OUT OF CONSCIOUSNESS. HER BODY showed signs of malnourishment, visible in slight loss of muscle definition. She didn't know her name, didn't know what day it was, who was president, where she lived. The poor thing was nonverbal and struggling to so much as move her arms. She appeared to be restrained by a hefty set of invisible chains.

The EMTs called the hospital in Fort Mojave over walkie-talkie just before nestling her into a stretcher and loading her into the ambulance. They left in a flourish of flashing lights, but not in the kind of rush someone gets when they're bleeding out.

The Needles sheriff's department was short staffed due to budget cuts and a bad reputation. Sheriff Spooner despised local government for dropping the ball on providing the money for a decent staff. Seemed money was going to every public service *but* law enforcement at a time when law enforcement was such high priority. The sheriff's department's reputation suffered from a town that, for the most part, had little respect for the law. The meth epidemic was staggering, which fueled home invasion and vandalism. A lot of people passed through Needles on their way to Laughlin, but few stopped for more than a fill up at the gas station and maybe a bite to eat at Denny's. Spoon Man figured if the town didn't look like a ghetto maybe people wouldn't be so damn scared off.

Due to budget restrictions there were only seven officers on staff, which meant only five were on the clock. Spooner already requested that the two officers enjoying a sweltering day off be called in. It was rare there was this kind of commotion in Needles. Generally they dealt with the same old drug and domestic violence calls sprinkled with the occasional car wreck or vandalism.

Deputies Gretch and Florence were questioning Matt and Sammy about the girl. Deputy Gretch was a Needles veteran who had her eyes on Spooner's position, but suspected that she was being held behind because of her gender, though she would never dare say anything about it. She had a hard stance on criminals that earned her the title of That Bitch Cop by local tweakers, which was fine by her. She had a heart of steel when dealing with lowlifes, but that steely heart could melt into a puddle when dealing with children and the infirmed, people struggling and in need. Deputy Florence too was looking at Spooner's badge, and he figured he had it clenched due to seniority, though he had been a big part of the department's suffering reputation. He had old school sensibilities, though at forty-two he hadn't even worked in an old school world. Came from his father working as a cop in Bullhead City back in the days when the west was wild and people turned a blind eye to roughing up some lawless thug. The kind of thing that Florence tried to get away with whenever he could, which was easier before he was partnered up with Gretch, who, despite being known as That Bitch Cop, was pretty disciplined and reserved, at least in his mind.

Matt and Sammy explained that they were on their way to Lake Havasu when they decided to check out the mud caves.

"Wait a minute." Deputy Florence wrinkled his brow in confusion. "I'm not following. You just *decided* to veer off the highway in hundred plus degree weather to look at, what, something called mud caves?"

Sammy nodded. Matt said, "Yeah, man, the Mojave Mud Caves. We were just poking around when this girl walks out all dazed."

Florence pursed his lips. "Mud caves? What gives you the idea there'd be mud out here in the desert?"

"Saw it on the Internet."

"Saw it on the Internet," Florence mocked. "I bet you'd walk off a cliff if you saw it on the Internet."

Deputy Gretch was clearly irritated with her partner, but she had to remain professional and slip into the good cop role that Florence couldn't pull off if he tried. "Was anyone else with you?"

Sammy nodded. "Yeah. Nikki, Ollie, and Shawna. Shawna got herself lost or something."

Gretch offered a questioning look. "Where are they?"

"Still out there," Matt said.

Florence piped in. "I'm not getting this. So they stayed behind and you drove this girl here? Is that it?"

"Yep. She needed medical attention. We had to."

"They have a car then, I assume."

"No. I said we'd send help. That's what I'm trying to get you to understand. Shawna got lost and we found this girl. We have to get back there. Hopefully they've found her."

Gretch, mouth slightly agape, eyes wild, said, "But it's at least a hundred ten out there. You left them in this heat? What's wrong with you?"

"We left them with a cooler full of water. Besides, the temperature inside the mud caves is better, and it's shady."

"Mud caves," Deputy Florence muttered with mild disgust.

Fifteen minutes later, after Matt and Sammy received a full

pat down, all four of them were piled into a sheriff's SUV. Matt and Sammy sat in the back, divided from the deputies by thick wire mesh. To their relief they didn't have to be cuffed for the ride. They weren't under arrest "yet" Florence said as he closed the back door. Sammy and Matt shared a worried glance. They hadn't done anything wrong, but trusting the police was something neither of them could easily stomach. After Matt's military stint he developed staunch anti-establishment beliefs.

By the time they got there night had fallen, but the moon shone high and bright, nearly full and glowing an almost toxic shade of orange. Matt directed Florence, who was driving the vehicle, on where to turn off of the highway. At the end of the road Florence put the SUV into four-wheel drive and cut through the soft desert sand to the area where the mountain split.

"Through that opening. It opens up to a valley with mountains on all sides. That's where the mud caves are. You can see them in the mountain walls. It's pretty trippy."

Florence shook his head and offered Matt a hardened glare. "Trippy? This is serious, you leaving friends out here like this. If they're in danger it's on you, got that? I will hold you responsible to the last letter of the law."

Deputy Gretch sighed. "Come on, Tim, they haven't done anything wrong."

"Yet."

"Look," Matt said, "we had no choice. Like I said, Shawna went and got herself lost. Ollie and Nikki stuck around to look for her and we said that we'd send help. Here we are."

Deputy Florence pulled his service revolver. "You two lead the way and don't try anything funny, got it."

Deputy Gretch shot Florence a contemptuous look. "That's not necessary."

"We don't know they're not trying to ambush us or something. Can't be too careful."

"We'll lead the way, no prob," said Matt. "We're not armed. You checked us, remember? You really gotta point that gun at our backs?"

Deputy Florence, growing more agitated and defensive by the second, gestured toward Matt and Sammy. "Just get a move on. Just so long as you're truthful, you have nothing to worry about."

"Easy for you to say. You don't have a gun pointed at you."

Matt and Sammy led the two cops into the mountains, but they didn't make it to the mud caves before a shadow descended upon them.

Chapter 10

Brandy wasn't home when Big Vic got back from hours driving around town and even into Fort Mohave. He hoped she would be there, waiting for him, worried about where he had been, but he knew better. She would have called. Problem was, he didn't know a whole lot about her past, the people she had spent time with, done drugs with, got blackout drunk with. It was a lifestyle Vic wasn't familiar with. He'd have a drink here and there, but life on the road rarely afforded him with that luxury. A DUI would ruin not only his career, but his life. Besides, he never understood the appeal of taking substances that killed inhibition. He'd seen the negative affects enough to learn from the examples of others.

His ex on the other hand, she was probably responsible for edging Brandy toward the seedy side of the human condition. When Vic and Amanda split, he hit the road and she spread her legs like peanut butter. It was no life for his daughter to live, seeing all the men in and out of the house, having her first drink, her first toke at such a young age, but Big Vic was a trucker. It was in his blood. It was the only way he knew how to make a living.

Sometimes he loathed that fact.

Sometimes Vic wondered if things would have turned out differently had he chosen a different profession, something nine to five that would have kept him in town with his family.

Then again Amanda would have probably cheated anyway. Way Vic saw it, a cheater was a cheater. It was bound to happen. Nothing he could have done about it.

Vic rarely thought about Amanda, and he certainly didn't think about how their lives could have been different. With Brandy missing, it was natural for his thoughts to go there. As much as he loathed doing so, Vic stopped by her mobile home while out looking for his daughter. He figured maybe Brandy went back to her mother, though he couldn't see why. Brandy had shared with him her reason for leaving, that one of Amanda's asshole boyfriends tried to molest her and her mother took *his* side. Vic was fit to burst when he heard that. He demanded the asshole's name, but Brandy couldn't remember. Good thing, too. Vic would have looked him up and beat the shit out of the poor sod. Probably would have spent a night or two in jail for assault and battery. Wouldn't be the first time, though he considered his rough and tumble style of dealing with certain people to be justified, considering he only served knuckles to those who harmed the ones he loved.

Amanda was drunk. It was such a sad sight for Vic to see. As bad as things had gotten between them, he remembered the good days. Seeing her the way she was made him feel deep pity. She was really letting herself go. Just succumbing to the cheapo cigarettes and bottom shelf vodka. Maybe even meth. Amanda said she hadn't seen her daughter in years.

Vic had no reason to think she was lying. Brandy's hatred toward the woman who gave birth to her was a deep wound that never scabbed over much less healed.

Vic grabbed a beer from the fridge and stood there looking out the window above the sink, sipping and thinking,

thinking and sipping. He swiveled his head every so often, eying the door to Brandy's room. Had she been gone long enough to constitute checking her room? Would he be breaking some kind of father-daughter boundary in doing so? These were questions no dad wanted to ponder. Vic was comfortable with the contours of his mind, having spent so many hours at the wheel. After he found out about Amanda cheating he thought through the entire ordeal from Arizona to Florida and back. He saw things clearly then, but he had time to think. He had all the time in the world when blacktop rolled by in a blur. It wasn't quite as easy to deal with his problems here in the kitchen. His thoughts were turning inward, the possibilities dire. Big Vic cared about his daughter. As much as he held Amanda responsible for what became of Brandy during her Lost Years, he was just as much to blame, and he knew it. He lived everyday to amend the negative consequences of leaving his little girl in a madhouse.

After the second beer (which was about all Vic would consume on an average evening), his thoughts drifted to what happened at the sheriff's station. The woman who was brought in. The fact that Walt knew her name. What was up with that? Vic wasn't one to believe in coincidence.

He sure would like to know what Walt was doing tonight. Did he leave town? Was he rolling around in his ice cream truck selling dope to kids all done up nice in ice cream wrappers?

Does he know where Brandy is?

Where she's buried?

Big Vic broke his own rule and had a third beer. He stared at the door to Brandy's room as he drank and thought of Walt, his little girl, and mud caves.

CHAPTER 11

THE APPROACHING SHADOWS WERE CAST FROM A BRIGADE OF wasps overhead. At the sight of Matt and the others they shifted and swooped down one by one, the fingers of their many hands poised, stingers shining in the sun like deadly spikes that could impale a human with ease. Matt and Sammy dropped to the desert floor. Gretch and Florence assumed a shooter's stance, pointing their pistols to the sky and letting off shots.

"What the fuck?" Deputy Florence said. A wasp swung down, causing Florence to kneel so low that he rolled onto his back, never removing his aim from the beasts. He trained a bead on the head (it had a humanoid face!), and fired. The bullet hit the thing in the top right of its head, which brought it off balance. Its wings stopped buzzing and the wasp mutation dropped, quick and heavy, smashing into a cluster of rock.

The buzzing was like a group of prop planes overhead, only they could turn on a dime and swoop down with terrifying precision.

"What the hell is this?" Gretch said. She was being more

conservative about the rounds she fired, choosing only to shoot at human wasps that were direct threats.

Footsteps distracted the deputies. It was Matt, screaming and yelling and hightailing it out of the canyon via the trail they used to enter the place.

"Where you think you're going?" Florence yelled.

"Forget him!" said Gretch. "We have to deal with this first."

"He's going back to the SUV!"

Recognition hit Gretch and she dropped her gun. Matt was out of sight. Gone. The keys were in the SUV, keeping the AC cranked for the return trip home. It looked like Matt would be making that felonious trip solo.

A wasp hovered low and reached out to grab Gretch with its many hands, but she maneuvered herself in a sort of roll and slipped out of the thing's grasp. From the corner of her eye she saw Sammy crawling across the desert floor like an injured lizard. Gretch turned her head at the sound of a scuffle just in time to see a wasp thing drop onto Deputy Florence. Hands grabbed him. The slender, elongated abdomen was poised, jabbing Florence's leg with a stinger. Florence screamed (a sound so foreign to his normally alpha demeanor), and let off a few shots, but his body quickly fell limp. The gun dropped into the sand and the wasp took to the sky clutching the deputy's body.

"No!" Gretch aimed her pistol, but hesitated for fear of hitting her partner by mistake. At the height the wasp had flown, Florence would have fallen too far anyway. He would have broken bones, broke his spine, maybe fractured his skull. Gretch had always harbored resentment toward Florence due to his attitude and wielding of power due to the badge on his chest, but they had bonded over the past couple of years. It was hard to watch him carried away like that. It was hard to have hope when some grotesque, winged creature just flew away like her partner was nothing more than a piece of garbage.

The wasps were thinning, but Gretch was still a target. She tried to conserve her ammunition, but the urge to unload her pistol into the monsters was strong. Florence had done that. He might have been partially responsible for his own capture.

A humming intensified from behind. The buzzing of their wings was fairly intense, especially when one of them was barreling in on a victim. Deputy Gretch turned and saw the thing coming straight for her. Its wings flapped in a blur, its human-like face staring straight at her with grotesquely over-sized eyes and a pair of antennae like the type that used to protrude from old cars to pick up radio signals.

Deputy Gretch drew her pistol, aimed, and fired. The bullet didn't hit the ugly face, but tore through one of the arms and damaged a wing. The sheer velocity of the thing caused the writhing body to scream forward with such force it plowed into the mountain side, leaving it a contortion of crushed skull and twisted limbs. Blood gushed from the damaged cranium, pooling in the dirt to create a syrupy mud.

"Hey!" came a voice. Gretch spun around in search of the voice. "Over here!" It was Sammy. He had found a cluster of rocks to hide behind. The idea of taking refuge with one of the boys she and Florence had taken out there (a pair they secretly held in contempt and scrutiny as perpetrators of potential crimes) was preposterous. In most situations.

Careful not to trip over rogue rocks, Gretch crossed the space between her and Sammy. "Get in here!" Sammy said. The opening to the rocky shelter was slender. Gretch took off her utility belt in preparation, but it didn't look good. Sammy was a wiry guy who Gretch would have pinned for a stoner, the type who was still young enough to have a metabolism that was good enough to fend off the late night junk food binges brought on by epic cases of the munchies.

Hands first, Gretch reached into the slender opening and attempted to maneuver her way into the tight safe-haven. Sammy grabbed her hand to assist, which brought on a defensive reaction (in her mind he was still regarded as a potential danger), but Gretch allowed him to help. Slipping her torso between the rocks was tight (especially considering the bulletproof vest and gear she wore), but with Sammy's assistance, she was going to make it. Suddenly there was pressure on her feet. Gretch let out a sound that was somewhere between a scream and a yell.

One of the wasp creatures had a grip on her legs. She was in no position to look back, but she could feel the hands. Several sets of them with a grip fit to break bones.

"Oh shit!" Sammy said. "It's got you!"

Gretch attempted to kick her legs, but the thing had too strong a grip on her. Sammy let go of her arms and reached through a gap in the rocks for her utility belt. Deputy Gretch's body went slack, fear entering her eyes in that moment as Sammy pulled the belt into the small cave. The wasp thing yanked and she slid out a few feet before using her arms to brace herself within the rocks.

Sammy pulled her gun. He shook his head, mouth agape. "Don't worry. I would never do something like this normally." He handled the firearm like he'd never even touched one before, like the weight of the thing was surprising to him. Crouching, Sammy found a good gap in the rocks and pointed the gun at the wasp creature. The thing stood on multiple legs, slender yet tightly muscled, posed in a defensive stance. Its massive abdomen protruded from behind like a huge malformed black balloon, the stinger, thin and pointed like a rattlesnake's fang, poised and glistening with a bead of poison. Four arms or so reached out, grabbing at Gretch and yanking her legs. Sammy fingered the trigger. The blast from the barrel thrust him backward. Rocks dug into his spine and the back of his head. The range of the shot was close enough that Sammy's inexperience wasn't too much of a hindrance. The bullet nailed the wasp, ripping a hole in its upper abdomen, which pierced the beast, popping through the back in a spray of blood and pus-like fluids. The beast let go of Gretch and went limp.

Sammy set the gun down. His hand shook like he had Parkinson's. Gretch slid her legs into the hideaway and snatched her gun. She hesitated as if she considered pointing the firearm at Sammy, but decided he wasn't a threat.

"What the hell are those things?" Sammy said. He just sort of stared off through the gap where he took his shot. The wasp twitched, its respiration slowing as life fled its body along with a myriad of fluids that smelled like minerals. The arms and legs, human in design yet covered in coarse black hairs and hinged strangely, curled up like the appendages of a dead spider.

"You tell me," Deputy Gretch said.

"They weren't here before. We found that girl, and—" Sammy was interrupted by a sharp jab in his back. His face scrunched up. "Oh fuck!" he pulled himself away and turned just in time to see the huge stinger through a gap in the rocks, glistening with his blood. The ass end of the wasp gyrated, waving the stinger around like a conductor's baton.

Sammy joined Gretch against the wall of the mountain where the wasps couldn't get to them. "Jesus it hurts," he said. "Goddamned thing shanked me."

"It looked like a stinger," Gretch said. "Try to calm down and breathe, okay."

Sammy's body slackened. "I'm not feeling so good."

Gretch grabbed Sammy's shoulders to keep him from falling over. "The poison."

"'Oison?" Sammy was hardly able to speak. Vomit spilled out of his mouth and nose in a cascade down the front of his shirt.

Gretch reared her head back, bumping a rock. The smell of

vomit was powerful. She spoke with a hand over her nose and mouth. "The wasp's poison."

"Numb . . . "

"Oh shit." Gretch positioned Sammy in a way that held him upright. She then grabbed her utility belt and pulled the walkie talkie. She pressed the button several times. No signal. "Dammit!"

Sammy stared at her, his eyes glossing over. He didn't do so much as twitch. The stinger that had jabbed Sammy through a gap in the rocks flicked this way and that. Eventually giving up the search for something soft and fleshy, that particular wasp creature gave up and flew away, perhaps assuming the threat it was after had been extinguished.

CHAPTER 12

Nikki had been lying in a pile of warm bodies. After managing to move her limbs and free herself from the suspended state of paralysis the poison had caused, she stood there staring at the unfortunates who had been captured before her. They stared back, eyes bloodshot and leaking tears over glistening, dirty faces. They all looked at her like she could do something to help them. Some of them, the ones closer to the bottom of the pile, were dead, their skin discolored and leaking putrescent bodily fluids through facial orifices or cuts and tears in their skin. Whiffs of their stinking death mingled with an ammonia reek of urine and powerful body odor.

Nikki spoke in a whisper: "I swear, I'll bring help. I'll do what I can to help you." She couldn't think of anything else to say. Words were empty in a hell like this.

How long these unfortunates had been there. Were they even sane or were they staring off into the Big Empty? If they were lucky shock will have set in and eased them from the torment of a slow, tortuous death.

Nikki had to look away. She couldn't bear to go down that rabbit hole if she was going to get out of this place.

The cave was dim. The only light came from two openings in the wall of the mountain. At this point Nikki's eyes had adjusted enough that she could see clearly, though there were innumerable shadows and dark depths like empty chasms. Most of the wasp creatures had fled for reasons she could only speculate. She was no fool. They would be back.

Sticking to the shadows, Nikki crept slowly as not to disturb any of the remaining wasps. Some of them were crouched close to the cave floor as if sleeping, others crawled up and down the walls of the cave, but nothing made any sense to Nikki. She tried to ascertain a pattern to their behavior, but their movements appeared random, agitated. Nikki didn't want to alert them for fear of getting another dose of poison or worse. The faces were human, and the many arms looked more akin to Homo sapiens anatomy than that of an insect, though they were slender and black and covered in coarse hair. What kind of teeth did the beasts have? Were they capable of conscious thought? Just what the fuck were they doing here?

After watching the behaviors of the wasp things for a while, Nikki came to the realization that she was flat out terrified. Mesmerized she watched the wasps crawl around, taking flight in and out of the holes in the mountain wall. Then she saw one emerge from a dark hole within the cave itself. The wasp thing that crawled from the interior hole was a bit smaller than the others, the size of a large breed dog whereas the others she'd seen were the size of large humans. The black of its abdomen was pale and the face was white, almost translucent, the skull showing beneath the thin layer of skin. Its eyes were large and cataract, as opposed to the black eyes of the other wasps. Nikki couldn't help but notice that this smaller wasp had some sort of dark grue on its lips, as if it had been eating chocolate or blackberries.

The newcomer was slow, crawling on its fungus-white limbs like it was gaining its bearings. Like a newborn foal.

There wasn't a whole lot of activity from the hole in which the newcomer emerged, but the more Nikki's eyes adjusted to the dark, she realized that the hole was a part of some massive nest made of compact mud. It was constructed against the rock at the rear of the cave.

Mud wasps?

The new wasp used a sickly elongated tongue to wash its humanoid hands, licking the pale flesh and rubbing the skin across its face in quick, jerky movements. It tested its wings, intermittently fluttering them at blinding speed as if the thing couldn't synch them up for flight just yet. The young wasp moved along, deeper into the cave,

The nest commanded Nikki's attention like a secret in the cave of the damned. She'd seen mud wasp nests before, tucked into the eaves of her house. Small things that would be able to fit in the palm of her hand, seemingly harmless. Just bugs. She'd always felt that the mud wasp nests were more harmless than paper wasp nests. The latter variety always seemed to be swarmed with wasps. Those were the type she remembered her father spraying with a foamy aerosol poison like they were some kind of serious threat. The little mud wasp nests, however, were just sort of forgotten about as if docile and harmless.

Seeing a mud nest of this size was shocking and enticing all at once, and Nikki couldn't deny the urge to investigate no matter how absurd it seemed in a moment such as the present.

Keeping to the back wall of the cave, Nikki slowly inched her way toward the huge nest. The wasps on the ceiling didn't move, not in a threatening way anyhow. They continued their seemingly random and jerky maneuvers, the cleaning of their many hands with long, thin tongues. Was it sound that would attract their attention? Movement? Nikki didn't know, and she didn't want to find out, and yet she couldn't resist the urge to see what was inside the nest.

Nikki approached the smoothed out hole in the side of the nest from which the new wasp had crawled out. She craned her head for a tentative look inside afraid of what she might see and yet filled with some absurd awe. It was dark. The nest wasn't a place for light. From within she heard low, agonized moaning. Pain. Suffering. Human suffering, like what one expects in the emergency room in the wake of nuclear fallout. The sounds from within caused Nikki great reservation and fear that radiated through her body like waves of adrenaline.

Primal urges told her to flee, but the sounds were unmistakably human. She glanced back from where she had come. How the hell did all of these people end up in here? She was beginning to fear that she would never get out. If these people hadn't managed to get out how could she expect to?

Nikki leaned her head into the nest for a better look. Agonized moaning filled her ears, but the dark was too deep for her eyes to pierce. She just stared into the murk, eyes adjusting to a darkness deeper than they had already adjusted to in the cave, and then she saw something that threatened to pull a scream from her lungs, a scream that would undoubtedly alert the various wasps lingering in the cave like loyal, sentient warriors in wait.

From behind, a sound like feet crunching on the cave floor issued. Startled that one of the wasps was behind her, Nikki faced her fears, faced the horror she had just seen, and entered the nest. It was even more cavernous than the cave itself, with tight chambers that were good for hiding, so that's what she did.

Her eyes were closed as not to see the horrors she had faintly witnessed before something snuck up on her, but her ears were open and the pained moaning was only intensified by her presence.

Matt's not coming back for you. He's already in Lake Havasu with a bleach blonde bimbo under each arm and a bottle of Coors in each hand.

Ollie didn't want to believe that, but his persistent mind droned on as he navigated the smooth tunnels like weaving his way through a dark and hopeless maze. He was deep within a mountain, and what was outside? A mile of desert between he and the highway? This fateful excursion felt more and more like a death sentence with every step, every drip of sweat off his shellacked face. He checked his phone from time to time, but all it was good for was the light it provided, and he had a flashlight that would suffice. Better to keep the remaining charge of the battery, just in case he turned it on and got a signal.

Ten minutes later and Ollie began to hear faint, indistinguishable sounds ahead, though there was no new light to speak of. He continued in the same direction, ears tuned to the sounds that slowly grew louder, a hum that he almost became used to even as it intensified, easing up on him like slowly wading into cool water.

A buzzing sound.

Finally the hollow tunnel opened up into a cave and the buzzing was evident in the presence of giant wasps. Ollie cut his light and softened his steps to avoid detection. He stood at the opening to the cave and observed the place as his eyes adjusted, which didn't take long since he had been in darkness for hours now. The cave was huge, with wasps on the ceiling, wings fluttering, twitching. Even small wasps were a bit of a threat, but this magnified version of a household pest was insane.

The gaping mouths of many tunnels like the one Ollie was standing at dotted the smoothed over walls like black dots, but more interesting was the massive mud nest at the rear of the cave. Ollie couldn't see too much detail, but it looked remarkably like the little mud wasp nests he had seen in the eaves of his house, only enlarged into something giant and alien.

Stunned and fearful, Ollie stood motionless, just watching the massive wasps in their jerky movements. They were huge with translucent wings, but stranger still were the rows of legs on either side that were human in structure, with hands at the ends. The head was a vile mutation of human and insect, flesh smooth with eyes like swollen black plumbs embedded in their faces, mouths torn open further than should be, serrated mandibles clicking together like some long lost bushman language. Listening to buzzing and the clacking of mandibles grated on Ollie's ears, but he was stunned, too afraid that he would catch their attention, for the most terrifying part of the humanoid wasp was the stinger. Those things had poisoned bayonets for weapons.

His eyes drifted through the huge chamber, attempting to make sense of what he was witness to. There were piles of debris pushed into corners, materials to beef up the intimidating mud nest. Wasps came and went through various caverns like good workers. Some came into the cave with clumps of mud in their human hands that were slathered into place on the huge nest and packed tight in a motion like a solitary game of patty cake. Where in the desert were they acquiring mud?

Ollie found his eyes fused to a strange pile off in a corner of the cave near where he stood. He stared so hard that he was looking through the pile, thinking about his fear, about how he could have possibly found himself in this situation. How did things go so wrong? That thought haunted him over and over like creeping regret. There was no cavalry that would rush in with giant cans of Raid, no fleet of helicopters that would blow the face off the mountain, no massive fly swatters to cream these monstrous things Ollie so feared. Soon enough his eyes lost their glaze and he was once again aware that he was staring at something horrifying, something that now came into focus as a pile of human bodies.

Ollie's skin rippled as if a frigid chill swept through the chamber. He could feel his heartbeat thrumming in his chest, and it seemed to bellow through a hollow shell of a body equal to the clanking of mandibles and buzzing of wings that almost faded into nothing as he stared at the bodies. The ones on the bottom of the pile were shriveled and rotten, limbs missing, green and black. The skin glistened in the faint light, beneath which was a dark saturation of wet rot. The ones on top were fresher, though they looked pretty bad off and it was hard to tell if they were breathing.

And then Ollie recognized one of them.

Shawna!

In that very moment as he understood that he was looking at his girlfriend's lifeless body lying atop a stack of death, the masses of wasps took to the air in an agitated flurry, and, one by one, they zipped out of the openings at the front of the cavern where the light of the stars and moon shone in. With their numbers diminished, Ollie crept the distance between he and the body pile and put his fingers to Shawna's neck for a pulse.

CHAPTER 13

NIGHT FELL ON THE SECOND DAY OF BRANDY'S DISAPPEARANCE. Big Vic wondered how he would have dealt with this had he been on the road. He wouldn't have known. His ex certainly wouldn't have made an effort to contact him. Same way he made little effort to let her know, though that was more because he knew she didn't give a shit. There was no need to open old wounds. She wouldn't help look for Brandy anyway.

But scars were reminders and scar tissue tore easily, as it did when Vic decided to enter Brandy's room and poke around a bit. It was the responsible thing to do, as much of a creeper as it made him feel to look through his daughter's things. Sure, he'd changed her diapers, wiped her ass, gave her baths when she was a baby (when he was home), but his little girl turned into a woman, seemingly overnight, and he was quite conscious of her space.

As Big Vic went through Brandy's possessions he was aware of how little he'd actually seen of her room. Their paths crossed in the living room or the kitchen. He had no reason to enter her room. He had always thought about her living with him like someone renting a room. He wouldn't dare intrude upon a tenant, and neither would he intrude upon Brandy.

Vic was no fan of mystery novels or television shows, so he didn't know what to look for. He figured he would know it when he found it, and something about the cigar box sitting on the shelf that was her bed's headboard caught Vic's attention. He remembered that Amanda had had a cigar box, and it hadn't been for cigars. He grabbed the box, judging nothing by its weight, and opened it. His heart dropped. How could he have been so stupid? How did he not see the signs? In the wooden cigar box was a glass meth pipe, rolling papers, lighters and unfolded paperclips with black ends.

Goddamn Walt!

There was no way for Vic to know for sure that it was Walt who got his daughter back on speed, but he most definitely contributed, and he was the last one to see her alive. Vic had tried to cut Walt a little bit of slack, but deep down he knew something was up. Walt was a slimy weasel. The kind of no goodnick who bullied kids going back to preschool and corrupted the weak minded. The kind of guy who didn't care if he was contributing to someone's bad habit. Didn't care if he was putting someone's life in peril just so long as he got what he was after.

Vic stared at the contents of the box for a couple of minutes before setting it opened on Brandy's bed. He clenched his fist. His blood pressure rose. He felt foolish in that moment, foolish for letting Walt get out of his sight, for allowing the son of a bitch the opportunity to flee, because now Big Vic was sure that Walt had something to do with his daughter's disappearance.

After a few moments processing his discovery, Vic jumped in his truck to cruise the seedier part of what was a pretty seedy town. He left a note on the coffee table just in case, by some twist of fate, Brandy were to come home while he was out.

A town like Needles pretty much went to sleep at sundown, at least the parts of town that passers by see on their way to Laughlin, but there was an underbelly that didn't sleep so much. Local residents knew the areas with bad reputations the way the police did, and locals kept away from those areas after dark if humanly possible. Big Vic figured if Walt was still around, that's right where he would be, and he should be fairly easy to find considering he drove a goddamned ice cream truck.

Vic was smart enough not to roll through the bad neighborhoods more than once for fear of arousing suspicion. With no ice cream trucks in sight he felt defeated, and then, just off the main drag, in the very abandoned gas station Walt said he last saw Brandy, Big Vic saw the ice cream truck. It was likely that there were more than just one ice cream truck in Needles considering the sweltering heat, but Vic was sure this one belonged to Walt.

Big Vic pulled into the abandoned gas station and cut the engine before he realized that he was interrupting a drug deal. He opened his door and saw, in the glow of the ice cream truck's lights, that there were three men, all looking at him with glassy bug-eyes. Vic hesitated, considering that he could close his door and peel out before things got hectic, but he was committed, and it was his daughter's safety that drove him forth. He would face serious danger to save her, and the only lead he had was this Walt punk.

"What the fuck are you doing here, pops," Walt said, his voice half dominant and half whiny as if he felt like he needed to keep his gruff armor in front of these bedraggled dope fiends even though he was intimidated by Big Vic.

Vic approached the trio with purpose. "Don't call me pops, you goddamned deadbeat tweaker."

"Who the fuck is this guy," one of the other tweakers said. He had a handlebar moustache and a sunken face with a dirty grin like he hoped some shit was about to go down so he would have an excuse to bust some ass. The other guy looked terrified, as if perhaps this was some kind of undercover sting.

"You need to back off," Walt said. "Face it, dude, Brandy ran off. She's probably hiding out somewhere. She was pissed off the other night."

Vic reached out and grabbed Walt's shirt collar, twisting the fabric in his tightly clenched fist and yanking him forward. "Then you're gonna show me where you think she might be."

Handlebar Moustache reached for Vic, muttering some kind of nonsense, but Vic, fueled by anger that scumbags such as these would gleefully reintroduce speed to his daughter, punched the guy in the face. Handlebar was caught off guard, his head jerking back with the weight of Vic's fist. He fell down, but jumped back up quickly. Blood started a slow trickle from his nose. He approached Vic again, only this time Vic used Walt's spindly frame as a battering ram, knocking Handlebar back on the ground. Big Vic then used his other hand to clinch the fabric of Walt's pants. He hefted the guy and threw him into his other friend like tossing a large log.

"My beef is with Walt," Big Vic said as he opened and closed his hand to alleviate the sting from Moustache's hard head. "If you're smart (that might be a poor choice of words), I'd clear out and leave us to our business."

Handlebar pulled himself from beneath the deadweight of Walt's body and stood on shaky legs. He looked at the other guy, who had seemed pretty shaken up from the beginning, and said, "Let's go, man." The other guy nodded and they took off into the hot blanket of night.

Walt, still lying on the ground, stirred. His head had hit the fractured asphalt pretty hard.

Vic pointed an accusatory finger at Walt. "I'm not letting you out of my sight until we find Brandy. If you know where she is you can say so at any time."

Walt looked up, eyes bloodshot and glistening. His head jittered like he was in the midst of a bad drunk. "I told you, pops. I don't know where she is."

Big Vic reached out his hand. The look on his face said that he was beginning to believe this asshole. "Then let's find her."

Walt hesitated before taking Big Vic's hand. "This is technically kidnapping. Right?"

Big Vic shook his head. "Wrong. You're helping me because you want to find Brandy as much as I do. Right?"

They held hands in a tight sweaty grip that teetered on the edge of one or the other bringing them into a full-blown fight, but after the way Vic managed the other two it would be foolish of Walt to engage the man, and he knew it.

Walt nodded and let go of Vic's hand. "Alright, Pops. But I don't even know where to start. She just walked off, man. Seriously. You gotta believe me."

Vic's face clenched up a bit. "I didn't at first, I got to admit, but . . ." he let it hang there, and Walt nodded as if maybe he was finally understanding the struggle and strife Pops was dealing with. "We'll take my truck," Vic said. "I have a hunch about something, something I overheard—"

Tires screeched like a falcon up the street cutting Big Vic off mid-sentence. He and Walt looked in the direction of the squealing tires to see a police SUV coming around the bend at high speed. It took out the corner of a sign from a dilapidated motel and was heading straight for Vic and Walt.

Vic's eyes grew. "Shit!" He and Walt dashed away from the street and watched as the police vehicle narrowly missed a light post and clipped Vic's truck, which put the SUV into a spin. The thing went up on two wheels, but the driver managed to keep from flipping. When all four tires hit the street the vehicle fishtailed wildly and that's when the driver completely lost control, smashing into a telephone pole.

The instinct to help filled Vic and he ran to the wrecked

car, temporarily forgetting the man he planned on taking hostage for a time. Steam hissed from the radiator as small tufts of smoke coughed from the engine. The driver's side door opened and a man got out. He had a cut on his head that was bleeding down half his face, and he moved like someone losing their sea legs.

"Take it easy," said Vic, and then he realized the man wasn't wearing a police uniform. "Wait a minute. What are you doing driving a cop car?"

The guy shook his head. "Wasps," he said, almost choking on the words. "There are wasps coming. Huge wasps." He looked back the way he came, eyes in the sky.

"You're in shock."

"Bullshit! They're coming!"

That's when a low buzzing filled the sky like a fleet of bombers preparing for an invasion.

Big Vic's eyes went northward, his brain struggling with the realization that this man with blood cascading down his face wasn't hallucinating, for indeed the sky was filled with a blanket of impossibly huge wasps. And they were getting close, the sawing buzz of their arrival increasing with their approach.

"We gotta get away!" said Matt.

Vic's truck was too mangled to drive. Wasn't worth trying in a high-tension situation such as this, so he dashed for Walt's ice cream truck. "Walt! Give me your keys!"

Matt followed Vic while Walt just stood there, transfixed with the creatures in the sky. He shook his head slowly. "I must be trippin'."

Matt opened the sliding door on the side of the ice cream truck and got inside. He crouched between the driver and passenger seats yelling for Vic and Walt to *come on! Come on!*

Big Vic had his hand on the driver's side door handle, but hesitated. "Goddamn it!" He stomped across the sandy asphalt and grabbed Walt by the shoulder, turning the stunned man around. "What the hell are you doing?"

"I must be trippin', man."

"Come on! We have to get out of here, you fucking psycho! I'd let your dumbass just sit here and get mauled by those things, but I need you. Gimme your fucking keys and get into the goddamned van. NOW!" Big Vic leaned in and yelled that last word into Walt's ear. He had become worked up, breathing heavy, face reddened. He had to watch it, considering his blood pressure. Last thing he needed was to drop of a heart attack.

Walt snapped out of his daze, mechanically pulled the keys from his pocket and placed them in Vic's open palm.

Vic said, "Come on!" and then ran for the ice cream truck.

A wasp broke from the pack and dropped quickly, zeroed in on Walt, who screamed and went into a full run. Big Vic opened the driver's side door and got into the ice cream truck. He put the key into the ignition and cranked the engine. Foot on the brake, Vic put the truck into drive, prepared for a quick departure.

Walt ran, but the wasp propelled through the sky like a missile. Walt's foot caught a patch of loose gravel and he went down hard. The massive wasp thing zoomed over his body, the many hands grabbing at Walt's clothes, but only getting enough purchase to slide his body a few feet along the asphalt, grinding his chin and elbow into road rash. Walt jumped to his feet. Dazed, he patted his face and picked off gravel that had turned to raspberry jam with his blood.

Big Vic was in full-blown adrenaline-fueled panic mode. "Get in, god damn it!"

Walt snapped out of his daze and got into the back of the ice cream truck.

CHAPTER 14

SAMMY'S BODY HAD BECOME COMPLETELY SLACKENED AND unresponsive from the wasp sting. Gretch tended to him as best she could, first as a sheriff, and then more as a nurturer, as was her nature. Seeing the young man in distress reminded Gretch of her own son, Brandon, though he was only twelve years old. He would be Sammy's age in no time, and probably venturing with his friends to lakes and caves and deserts and canyons for innocent fun. At least Gretch liked to think her son would lead a good life and enjoy innocent pleasures, but she was no fool, and she had seen enough young people and their proclivities to know that they pretty much all did something that would make their parents cringe. Some were worse than others, that's all. She herself had done some stupid things when she was young, bullet proof, and ten feet tall.

Gretch felt for Sammy. She didn't know him from Judas, but he had done nothing on the drive out to rouse suspicion, and now, watching his eyes open and glassy and terrified, his body unable to move, she wanted to do whatever she could to help.

"Sammy, can you hear me?"

He just stared ahead, unblinking, unmoving, but Gretch could see something in those eyes. Recognition?

"Do you understand what I'm saying? Can you blink your eyes?"

Nothing. And yet . . .

Yes, he could hear, she could see recognition, fear in those eyes.

"You can understand me, I'm sure of it. I want you to know that I will do everything in my power to get us out of this, okay?" She nodded, maybe to give herself a sense of recognition.

One of Sammy's legs was twisted beneath the other in what had to be an uncomfortable position, but, with no way to maneuver himself or speak of his discomfort, there was no way to tell if he was in pain. Gretch grabbed his leg. It was like grabbing a huge salami. She pulled the leg from beneath its counterpart, maneuvering him into what looked like a more comfortable position. Gretch wanted to believe that she could see in his eyes that he was relieved, but really it was hard to tell. Those eyes were frightened, catatonic even.

"There, that's better," she said.

Outside of the cave the sounds of wasps had diminished in a rising desert wind. The space within the rocks was cramped, but Gretch was afraid that mere bullets weren't enough to protect her from the things she had seen out there. She had gotten into law enforcement to be on the right side of the law. She figured that if she was the one with the gun and the badge, she would develop a level of confidence that she lacked as a pedestrian, and she had been right about that. After training she felt empowered. Now, with giant human-like wasps in the air, the badge didn't mean shit, and the gun wasn't going to keep a nest of those things at bay.

From her utility belt Gretch drew a small fold-up binoculars. She placed them to her eyes, focusing on the valley seen through a gap in the rocks. Up the side of the mountain she could see two distinct caves where the wasps entered and exited with regularity. Through the lenses they almost looked small and harmless, but whenever she got a look at one of their faces or the human hands on those lacquer limbs that gently swayed with the flight patterns, she was taken aback, the reality of the situation sinking in even further. It felt as if they would converge an attack on her were she to slip out of the rock cluster. Gretch felt helpless.

After the years of working in law enforcement Gretch had shed a lot of the inhibitions she harbored as a young woman. Even off duty she walked with a sense of confidence, knowing full well how to deal with people were a dangerous situation to arise. It wasn't all about the gun in law enforcement, at least not in her eyes. The best way to deal with people issues was with her words, and she was good at that. Despite the bad reputation the police received across the country due to cop involved shootings and protests, Gretch had nurtured a relationship with the residents of Needles that, in turn, caused her to develop the confidence she had always found so hard to obtain before becoming a deputy.

The wasps, however, couldn't be reasoned with. This frightened Gretch more than anything. She hadn't felt this helpless in a long time. Though she was confident holding her own, she had learned to depend on Deputy Florence. They were a team (even if he sometimes clouted his alpha demeanor a bit too much), and she certainly could use his assistance right about now. The image of his body being carried away haunted her. Though he was a tough guy with that macho tough guy attitude, he'd always been afraid of heights. Gretch looked at Sammy, noting the terror in his eyes, the cognizance. If deputy Florence was cognizant when the wasp flew off, he must have been mortified.

Sweat poured down Gretch's face. The rocks, having sat in the sun all day, had absorbed enough heat to keep them warm all through the night. She unbuttoned the top of her shirt in a futile attempt at cooling off.

Gretch had tried her communications device (a fancy term for a walkie talkie), but she had no signal. Deputy Florence's band was all fuzz, and trying to reach the station did the same. Another side effect of budget cuts and small town life. Her phone was in the SUV. She didn't carry it on her due to the utility belt and the fact that her walkie talkie (communications device) was generally all she needed on the job outside of her lunch break and those times she and Florence were sitting in the SUV bullshitting while waiting for something to happen.

What about Sammy's phone?

In law enforcement Gretch was often called out to assist a male deputy for the purpose of frisking a female detainee for obvious reasons, but she had also frisked her fair amount of males. They didn't seem to mind, and she always asked if they would prefer a male deputy. It felt wrong to reach into Sammy's pockets for his cell phone, but these were extenuating circumstances.

"I know you can hear me. Well, at least I'm pretty sure you can. Look, I need to get to your phone. If I can get a call out, I can get help."

His eyes stared into hers. He blinked a few times, but it seemed involuntary, just a reflex to keep his retinas moistened. But she could tell that he was perfectly okay with her grabbing for his cell phone; after all, he had done the same with her gun, and that was a huge no-no. Extenuating circumstances indeed.

After fishing the cell out of his pocket, she was only mildly amused to see that he had a picture of a woman's bare breasts as the wallpaper. Fortunately he didn't have the thing locked, and Gretch wouldn't dare look at the photos. Just a call. If there were bars.

There was one bar.

Gretch punched 911. After a lengthy silence the phone rang. A woman answered. Was it Maria or Cat? Gretch couldn't tell because the connection was distorted, fading in and out. If Gretch remembered correctly, Maria worked the nightshift.

"Maria, it's deputy Gretch. Can you hear me?"

The voice on the other end was too distorted for Gretch to understand.

"I'm sorry, but I can't hear you. Deputy Florence and I are in trouble. I've lost communications. He was—" What could she say, that her partner had been taken by a giant wasp? That would sound absolutely bonkers. "One officer down. We're approximately seventy miles outside of Needles on the westbound forty. I have no idea if you can hear me, but we need medical help. Call into Laughlin for a helicopter to locate us. We're in the mountains."

Gretch was going to say more, maybe even drone on until her voice went dry, but the connection was lost. There was no way for her to tell whether Maria heard what she had said, and she wasn't even sure she gave all of the vital information.

She looked into Sammy's glassy eyes. "Help is on the way." Gretch didn't know whether she said that to comfort Sammy or herself.

Chapter 15

Momentarily forgetting the threat of giant wasps, Ollie knelt beside the pile of bodies and cradled Shawna's face in his hands. There was life in her eyes, terror, fear, however she seemed unable to move. Her face was slack, crooked almost unnaturally considering her position on the gruesome pile.

"Can you hear me?" Ollie asked.

Her eyes opened wide, which was as good as an answer. *Yes*, her eyes said, *I can hear you, but cannot move.*

Her head felt strange in his hands. There was no musculature to her neck. It was like a baby's head that, if not cradled correctly, would loll to the side snapping the spine, though Ollie assumed it would take more than that to snap a grown woman's spine.

Sounds in the cave drew Ollie's attention away from his girlfriend. The wasps were still scattered enough for him to help her without too much danger. At least that's what he told himself. Everything about this situation was dangerous and incomprehensible.

Ollie stood and grabbed the body that was lying atop Shawna's legs. "Here, I'm gonna get you out of this pile. We need to get out of this place."

Shawna's eyes were wide glass orbs, moving around in attempt to watch Ollie, terror-filled, as if worried that he would leave her there to die slowly in a pile of bodies all rotting together into a sticky sludge of human pâté.

Grabbing the body by a handful of shirt and pants, Ollie gritted his teeth and yanked the man off of Shawna. The body flipped over, facing the ceiling of the cave. A grunt came from the still mouth and Ollie could see that the man was conscious too, his eyes wide and frantic.

Ollie pulled his arms away, caught with a sudden fright. "Jesus Christ."

The man silently pleaded with Ollie, staring him straight in the eyes but unable to move so much as a pinky finger.

Ollie checked the cave for wasps. They must not have been disturbed by his movements, perhaps assuming that he was just another one of them, working over at the body pile. He looked into the man's eyes. "I swear, I'll be back if I can."

Gooseflesh rippled over Ollie's arms and legs causing a chill to dance up his spine, strong enough for him to physically shake. Other eyes were open, staring at him, pleading, crying, terrified. Some were dead—the ones on the bottom of the pile—but the others, all incapable of movement, just stared at him like he was their only hope. Faces were dirty and speckled with blood and saliva oozing out of slack-jawed mouths, dribbling into the eyes and noses beneath.

Ollie whispered, "What the fuck is going on here?"

The buzzing sound grew louder as some of the wasps that had fled the cave returned. This put a flame under Ollie's ass. He grabbed Shawna by the shoulders and gently slid her off of the other unfortunates. She was warm, and that was comforting, if there was any comfort to come of this. Even though her eyes were wild, Ollie had this absurd fear that she would be cold, that somehow her body had died and yet her eyes and brain lived on in some slow torturous death.

"I'm gonna have to drag you," Ollie said. "We need to get

into the shadows. I don't know what those things have you here for, but it can't be good."

The sound Shawna's legs made as they slid over the dirt floor was enough to attract the attention of several wasps. Ollie saw this and halted. He had no idea how a wasp saw the world. Was it a colorful multi-prism kaleidoscope? Black and white? Sonar like a bat? Did these things have the capability to think?

Ollie stood still, arms hooked under Shawna's armpits. He watched the wasps without moving, waiting for them to drift into their patterns before cradling Shawna and carrying her into the shadows. He positioned her on the ground, back against the curved cave wall. There was no way to tell whether she was comfortable or not. Her eyes had the same unblinking terror-stare she had while lying atop the body pile.

Ollie asked, "Can you move anything?"

Shawna stared back unblinking, but it was hard to tell whether she could even hear him, so he asked, "Can you hear me? Blink once for yes, twice for no? If you can."

She stared, face slack, drool beginning to seep from the corners of her mouth. Her breathing was shallow and wheezing. She appeared unable to blink, but she made an attempt, her eyelids moving as if trying to close but unable to. Her eyes glossed over and then a tear welled at the corner of one. Breaching her lashes it rolled down her face leaving a trail of moisture through a layer of dust on her cheek.

"You can hear me, I can tell," said Ollie. "Okay, I'm gonna get you out of here, but I have to find the way out. It's like a maze." Ollie closed his eyes for a moment, shaking his head. "Matt and Sammy went for help. I just hope they didn't forget about us. Nikki is missing. She was with me looking for you and then . . . and then we got attacked by some giant . . ." Ollie pivoted his head to look behind them. He had to look at those wasps again, just to assure himself that they were real. Giant, humanoid insects. Crazy. He drew in a deep breath and let it out in a lengthy sigh. "I have no idea what happened to her. Maybe she's in the body pile too."

The urge to scream was palpable. Nikki just about had to bite her knuckles. The odors alone were horrid. Rotting meat, blood, piss, shit, all twisted together like some rancid potpourri. She couldn't tell whether it was worse inside this tight tomb or out there with the giant wasps.

Nikki's eyes had adjusted some, helped along by light filtering in from the opening she crawled into the strange inner cave from. There were shapes in there with her. Human shapes, but no movement. It was like being in some kind of crypt, or like that underground mass grave in Mexico she had heard about where bodies are piled up when family can no longer afford to pay for a proper grave in the cemetery above.

Why did her mind insist on going there? This wasn't the time to think about mass graves.

The dim light faded. Nikki squinted her eyes at the opening from which she had come through. Staring back at her were the dead eyes of a human face that protruded like swelled egg yolks, only they were as black and shiny as polished onyx. Antennae sprouted from the forehead like rabbit ears on an old television. Mandibles wrapped around the face of the humanoid from the hinge of its jaw like a mutated extension.

Nikki froze, but her heart beat like crazy, pounding in her ears. She felt every vein in her body jumping. It was almost too much to take, but she was trapped and oh so vulnerable. There was nowhere to go. The thing just crouched there at the opening, looking in, its antennae twitching, mandibles clanking together. Tremors racketed Nikki's body, but she managed to keep herself under control by closing her eyes. It was better not to see the damned thing. Easier to keep some semblance of calm until the beast left.

She opened her eyes. The human wasp was gone. Nikki let out the breath she had been holding and closed her eyes again, this time in relief.

How much of this shit could she take? At which point did she lose it and run screaming, right into the clutches of one of those wasps, just to be stung and left in a pile of bodies?

And what were the bodies for anyway?

Fumbling around in the tight little inner cave, Nikki could feel limbs, a leg here, an arm there. Non-responsive dead weight.

Something moved. Nikki's eyes had adjusted better and she could see something beside her, some sort of form, a shape in the ground in the tight cocoon of mud. She knelt down and risked a hand to at least acquaint herself with the texture of the shape. Her fingers grazed something soft. She pulled them away before her mind registered that the texture was that of fabric. She held her hand out again and touched the shape. It was indeed clothing of some sort, soft like cotton.

She looked closer, trying to identify the shape knowing now that it was human. She could make out the legs, the skirt she had touched. The top half of the woman was unclothed. Her chest rose and fell with such delicacy it could very well be a trick of Nikki's eyes, a hallucination of wishful thinking. She knelt down onto her knees and edged forward, over the woman's legs, and then placed her hand on the woman's chest above her breast and she could feel the gentle weight of her breathing. Something like relief settled in for only a fleeting moment when the sluicing sound Nikki had heard returned, louder, closer, and then she saw it.

Nikki pulled her hand away from the woman. This time she couldn't stifle the yelp that seemed so loud within the tight confines of the mud cocoon. Gnawing and slurping on the woman's arm was a thing that lacked pigment. A ghastly little insect-like creature with the face of a grotesque, nightmarish baby. At the sound of Nikki's yelp, the thing stopped eating and looked directly at her with eyes that lacked color. Orbs like rain clouds. The translucent skin revealed the bizarre skull beneath that looked almost Cro-Magnon in its human-insect rendering. The woman's arm remained clutched in feeble little hands the color of jellyfish. On the thing's maw was a paste of blood, crusted over from multiple feedings.

Nikki stared at the thing, hoping it was as blind as it appeared. She dare not make a move, a sound for fear its other senses were heightened. After an excruciating thirty seconds the thing returned to its blood feast, noisily slurping and suckling at the ruined arm.

Body trembling, Nikki decided that it was better to face the wasps than their bloodthirsty larvae. She crawled backwards toward the opening from which she had entered, turning to see that she wasn't encroaching upon more larvae or the mothers and fathers who might be checking in on their young. All was clear. Nikki eased out of the hole in the nest and then crawled slowly to the back of the cave, into the shadows where she bumped into Ollie and, surprisingly, Shawna.

CHAPTER 16

As Big Vic pulled the ice cream truck onto highway 40 Walt was a mess. "You can't just take my truck, man!"

Big Vic didn't so much as avert his eyes from the road. "Like hell. You're in this with me. You can come clean any time you want."

"Jesus H., dude. I don't know where Brandy is. Where the fuck are you going? This is crazy!"

Matt, in the back of the ice cream truck, kneeling before the rear window, said, "Do you see any of the wasps?"

Vic craned his neck to see into the sky from the windshield. "Nothing now. They must have flown past us. Wasps? That really what those things are?"

Matt sat down on the floor in the back of the truck with his back against the rear doors. "I don't know. Looked like giant bees or wasps or something. It's a long story. Things weren't supposed to end up like this. It was just supposed to be a fun little detour."

"I recognize you from the sheriff's station. You came in with that girl."

Walt perked up, pivoting to look at Matt in the back of the van. "Delanie? Where the hell did she come from?"

Matt's normally self-assured swagger had been lost somewhere in the desert. He looked like a frightened child with muscles and tattoos. "The mud caves. Out in the desert. You know her? What the hell was she doing out there?"

Walt shook his head. "I met her a few times, but we weren't friends or anything. I don't know what the hell she was doing out there."

Big Vic looked at Matt through the rearview mirror. "What are the mud caves?" He then looked at Walt like he might also know of the caves and have something he'd like to get off his chest.

"Don't look at me, pops. I've never heard of no mud caves."

Matt asked Walt, "You got some water or something? I'm parched." Walt pulled a bottle of water from a package on a shelf beside the large cooler where ice creams bars of all colors, shapes and sizes were contained. He handed it over. "Thanks," Matt said and then he drank half the bottle in one prolonged guzzle. He took a deep breath and said, "The mud caves were something I heard about on the Internet, something to see in the desert. Seemed like a cool idea, but things got all fucked up. Now my friends are missing, those cops are dead, I think. Who knows? Hey, where you heading anyway?"

Big Vic shook his head. "Don't really know just yet. I'm looking for my daughter. Went missing. I saw you with that girl and I thought . . ." Vic blinked his eyes and cleared his throat, banishing the emotion that threatened to expose itself. "I thought that you might have found her, but, naw, some other girl. I got to thinking, though, and I'm wondering if there's some connection. You find some *other* missing girl out in the desert, maybe Brandy's out there. Needles isn't the greatest place on earth, but shit like this doesn't happen all that often. 'Sides, it's the only lead I have, and I can't stand just sitting around like she's gonna come walking through the front door like nothing happened."

"I don't know if we should go back there, man," Matt said shaking his head, eyes wide like he'd seen his own ghost.

"You said you got friends missing, right?"

"Well, yeah, but . . ."

"What kind of friend does that make you?"

Big Vic watched the road exchanging glaring glances at Matt through the rearview mirror. Vic had a face that was chiseled from rough granite, unpolished. He looked like he may have spent time in the pen and fought his way out of being anyone's bitch. He'd never been to prison though, but he certainly cut his teeth fighting all kinds of scum at various truck stops around the country.

"We're about an hour, hour and a half away," Matt said. "Keep heading up forty."

"So what's the deal with this girl you brought into the sheriff's station?"

Matt rubbed his hands over his face and sighed loudly, the way someone does when they want those around them to understand that they are weary or irritated. "Goddamn, man. It's like I'm in some fucking TV show, only there's no cliffhanger until next week. It just keeps going on and on." He took a moment, staring down as if the carpeted floor of the van would give him guidance, and then told Walt and Big Vic what happened at the mud caves.

Walt scratched his arms incessantly, grinded his teeth and chewing the insides of his cheeks. "Dude, you're trippin'. You're saying that chick came out of the rocks?"

"She was just sort of there," Matt said, eyeing Walt with contempt and disgust, for it was quite clear Walt was speeding, or perhaps coming down.

The open road was dark, illuminated by the dim headlights of the ice cream truck. Bugs zipped toward the lights like they had a death wish. Tractor trailers passed by going east, but there was no traffic going west. Vic pushed the truck forward at an even pace like blowing diesel across the country in his big rig, eyes set on the road, mind full of thoughts like the twisted roots of an ornery tree.

"The cave," said Big Vic. "She came from the cave. Had to."

"We were in the cave," said Matt. "I didn't see anyone."

"But you said there were a lot of caves, all over the mountainside." Big Vic nodded as if affirming his conclusion. "Yeah, that's where she is. In one of those caves."

Matt repositioned himself from sitting to squatting on his knees and reached for the lid of the ice cream cooler. "Mind if I have one of these ice creams?" he said as he opened the cooler.

Walt jumped up, but Matt saw the contents before he had a chance to close the lid.

"The fuck is this?" Matt said.

Big Vic's eyes flashed anger and concern in the rearview mirror. "What is it?"

Matt opened the freezer lid so that the hinge locked. He stared in at the contents, shaking his head. "You gotta be fucking kidding me. I can't get a break. Here I am, on parole, trying to do the best I can, and look at this shit! Just LOOK at this." He shook his head.

Walt grabbed the lid and slammed it down as if in doing so the knowledge of what was inside the ice cream freezer would vanish from Matt's head.

In complete control of the truck, Big Vic turned to look in the back, unable to see anything. "What is it?" he demanded.

Walt scratched at his neck like he was trying to get to his spine. His jaw was working overtime. The air in the truck was cool, but he was sweating like an HVAC guy working in an attic in August.

"Meth!" said Matt. "Fucking meth. Fucking Christ, man! I don't know if I should have you drop me off or what. If this rust bucket gets pulled over I'm going to be arrested and thrown back in the clink. Guilt by fucking association. Goddamn!"

Matt stood up as much as possible, pacing the back of the van. He placed his hands on the freezer to brace himself, and then pulled them back quickly. "Fingerprints. Dammit! How stupid."

"Don't worry about it," said Big Vic. "There ain't no cops on this road at night. Not even in the day, most the time."

"But what if?"

"He's right," Walt said.

"Shut the fuck up, you junkie piece of shit. Just fucking look at you. You're all fucked up."

Walt became defensive. "Watch it, asshole! I'll fuck you up—"

The van went into a screeching stop so abrupt that both Matt and Walt flew forward. Big Vic slammed the gear shifter into park and pushed in the emergency brake with his left foot. He turned around and directed his vehemence to the methhead and the meathead.

"Okay, no one's fucking anyone up unless it's me fucking you up. Got it? There's a lot more important shit going on right now than a little meth in a fucking ice cream truck. My daughter's life is on the line." He looked into Matt's eyes. "You have friends in danger, and you're gonna piss your pants about getting popped by the cops. You just took a drive with the damned sheriff. You ain't got nothing to worry about. And you," he looked into Walt's bloodshot, shifty eyes. "I could see you were a fucking doper loser from the day I met you. That's why I didn't like my daughter seeing you, but what the hell can I do. She's a woman. She wants to fuck her life up with some half-wit meth head, what can I really do about it?

"Thing is, I believe you when you say you don't know what happened to her. I been up and down every goddamned highway in the wonderful country of ours, dealt with all walks of life, the good, the bad, and . . . " Vic raised his eyebrow and tilted his head toward Walt, "the ugly. I know a liar when I see one. You're a liar for sure. All addicts are. That's why I can tell you're *not* lying about Brandy."

Matt became visibly anxious, continually checking the little windows in the back doors. "You think it's a good idea sitting here in the middle of the highway?"

Big Vic shrugged. "Someone comes along, they'll pass us. I wouldn't worry too much about it."

"What about the fucking meth, man? Are you not worried we'll get popped? What are you gonna tell the cops? They won't believe you."

Vic unbuckled his safety belt and squeezed between the bucket seats into the back of the ice cream truck. Without a word, he approached the freezer and opened the lid. His eyes blew up like he was witness to a gleaming stack of gold bars. His head pivoted to face Walt, who was crouched against the side doors with the window that slid open to do business with the little kiddies. Vic shook his head. "Christ, boy. You must be supplying all of Needles."

Walt couldn't help but crack a grin, as if that was some kind of time-honored accomplishment. "Supply and demand, man."

Big Vic let the freezer lid slam shut with a *thud*. "You the one turned Brandy back onto this shit?"

"No. I met her at someone's house one night. She was high already. I knew of her (who doesn't, right?), but that was the first time I met her."

Big Vic nodded. "You thought she was a slut, thought maybe you could get some, that it?"

Walt's calming demeanor tightened up as if he was terrified of how to answer this accusatory question. The pause indicated guilt. Vic nodded again. "Your poker face is for shit."

Walt pleaded, "Look, pops, really, you gotta—"

"Goddamn it!" Big Vic erupted like some demon swelling within his being had come to a head and popped. "Don't you fucking call me pops again. You hear me? I ain't your pops, motherfucker. I don't even *like* you. I know what you wanted with my daughter. I'm not *stupid*. You might have met her in a weak moment, but you plied her with your filthy dope and now what? She's gone. And I put that on you."

As if putting a cherry on top of that statement, a horn blared as a lifted truck zipped by them, passing in the opposite lane of traffic. The passing truck caused the ice cream truck to waver violently. Matt grabbed his head and crouched like someone stepped on a damn landmine. Walt braced himself against the wall of the van.

"Aw shit!" said Matt. "Dude's gonna call the cops. Hit the road, man. We can't just sit here any longer."

"Calm down," said Big Vic. "You think that asshole is going to call the sheriff you're dumber than you look."

Matt's face tightened up into a scowl. "What did you say to me?"

"Knock off the big man act. You're not from around here. You don't know how things work, and you certainly aren't a good judgment of character. Guy that sped past us in the middle of the night honking his horn is just like you. Some meathead who would leave his friends in the middle of the desert with a bunch of goddamned giant *wasps* flying around. Don't even say a word. No one's kicking anyone's ass. We're going to find your friends, we're going to find my daughter, and we're all going to pull our weight. Got it?"

Matt softened a bit, though his eyes were aflame. He nodded. "Yeah, sure. Sorry about your daughter, dude." He glanced sidelong at Walt with an even fiery expression, as if launching silent accusations.

Walt just nodded and said, "Just get this thing on the road. The ice in that freezer will put us all in prison for years."

"Not us," said Big Vic. "We get popped and you're taking all the blame. That's your shit. I know people locked up for life in Arizona State who owe me a favor. You drag us into this I'll have them sodomize you with a lead pipe so you bleed to death out your ass."

Big Vic returned to the driver's seat, put the ice cream truck into gear and took to the highway.

CHAPTER 17

Ollie could only see faintly in the dim cave, but he knew immediately who crept from the shadows. "Oh my god! Nikki! I thought you were . . ."

Nikki, who had looked so put together and confident when they set out on their trip to Lake Havasu, was shaking like a serious drunk in a dry county. Her eyes, glossed over, almost vacant like a catatonic, dropped to Shawna leaning lifelessly against the cave wall. This snapped Nikki out of her funk. Her mouth dropped open and the faintest crack of a smile broke through.

"You found her?" Nikki said.

Ollie nodded. "Yeah, but she's in bad shape. Can't move. Can't talk. I think she's paralyzed."

"Did you . . .?" Nikki's attention wandered toward the body pile. Though it was very warm, she shivered. "We've got to get out of here." Nikki's voice took on a more pleading quality, almost frantic and half crazed. "I can't stand to be in here any longer. I'm going to . . . going to lose my shit if I have to stay in here any longer."

Ollie put a finger to his lips and shushed Nikki. "Quiet. Don't rouse them."

"You got her from the pile of bodies, right? Is that where she came from?"

Ollie nodded. "Yeah."

"I was one of those bodies. I couldn't move. Not so much as a finger." The shakes, of which had begun to subside, returned. "It was the most frightening thing—" Nikki looked back the way she came, toward the mud nest with the translucent larvae and the suffering humans that were its food. She shook her head. "This place is hell."

Ollie nodded. "Look, I've been watching the wasps, trying to figure out a way to get out. See up there," he pointed to the pair circular openings in the cave wall. "Wasps come and go from there. I think the light coming in is from the moon. That's our only way out. The tunnels are just as bad as a maze."

"What about the wasps?"

"They're fairly docile. They move around in an almost robotic sense, like they have a task and must perform that task."

"You don't think they'll attack? Are you crazy? That wasp in the tunnels stung me and took me away." Nikki pointed at Shawna. "It was the sting that did that to her. Did that to me too."

"So how did you start moving again?" Ollie gripped Shawna's hand tight, as if hoping for a response, an equally loving squeeze to assure him that she would be all right, that she would snap out of the paralysis and they could all escape together.

"I don't know. Meditation, mind power, something like that."

"Mind power? The fuck?"

Nikki shook her head as if trying to dispel what she said or was wary about discussing it. "I don't know. Just something I do to deal with claustrophobia." Ollie wrinkled his brow. "Hard to explain," she said, and then she looked over her shoulder at the body pile. From this distance in the dark it was impossible to see if their eyes were pleading, wet and alive and unable to move. "I don't see any one else getting up."

Still focused on the grisly pile, Nikki squinted. "Wait a minute. There's movement, isn't there?"

Ollie, too, squinted at the human pile. "Holy shit, I think you're right." He squeezed Shawna's hand again, but there was no response.

An agonized moan like someone waking into pain from anesthetic came out of the mound of bodies like a beacon that immediately attracted the attention of two wasps who immediately deviated from their worker bee behaviors. They swooped down onto the pile and began jabbing the bodies with their stingers until the moaning was put to rest. The wet sound like daggers puncturing slabs of meat was sickening. One of the stabs was fatal, having slid into someone's brainpan. Blood poured out of the hole, dripping onto the smooth floor of the cave.

"Jesus," Ollie muttered.

Nikki shook her head. "They're poisoning them, keeping them alive but immobile. Well, most of them."

"Why?"

She closed her eyes and took a deep breath. "You don't want to know."

"What are we going to do?" Ollie said.

"We're going to get out of here. Over there. Where the wasps come and go. Like you said, it's the only way. If we go back into the tunnels we'll be lost forever, or at least until one of the wasps comes along and stings us and then we'll end up in the pile, and then . . ."

"What about Shawn—" Ollie gasped. He struggled to keep his voice under control. "She moved her fingers!"

Nikki grabbed Shawna's other hand. "The poison must be

wearing off." She looked into Shawna's glassy eyes. "Can you hear me? Shawna, can you hear me?"

Shawna's tongue flickered in her slack mouth, movement that had not been seen since discovering her lifeless body.

"Listen to me, Shawna," Nikki said. "You can do it, I know you can. Just focus and try to move your hand. Grab my hand. Grab Ollie's hand. Just focus. You can do it."

Ollie squeezed Shawna's hand, willing her to respond. It was as if there were no huge wasps lingering throughout the cave, threatening to do to him what they did to his girlfriend. All that mattered was that Shawna was alive and moving, conscious and talking and ready to get the fuck out of this damned mountain. Screw Lake Havasu, screw Matt and Sammy, they would get out of here and hitchhike back to Southern California if they had to. It would be the last time either of them followed Matt on some half-baked idea of fun.

Something came out of Shawna's mouth like her vocal box was vomiting sound. Nikki put her hand to Shawna's mouth before she could let out one of those alerting moans that would have gotten them all injected with poison. "Shhhh. I know—It feels weird. Just be quiet and we can all get out of here."

Ollie said, softly, "Squeeze my hand, Shawna. Squeeze it."

And she did, however faint. It was enough for Ollie to beam, to find a slice of hope in the Cave of Doom. He looked at Nikki, eyes alight, but she didn't look quite so confident, so excited about this menial accomplishment.

"The wasps are laying low," Nikki said, "not as active. I don't know shit about how they function, but this might be the best chance we have at getting out of here. Looks like a lot of them have gone through the tunnels, and those over there are building a nest or something. There are a few clinging to the ceiling. Maybe they're guards or something, but they haven't noticed us."

"Shawna can't move yet," Ollie said.

"I think she's gonna have to."

Slowly Shawna began to move more than just her hands. She attempted to form words, but every time she did so, Nikki's hand covered her mouth.

"We can brace her," Nikki suggested. "At least until we get to the opening. By then she'll probably work herself back into her stride."

Ollie looked confused. "Well, what if she doesn't?"

"We can't sit here and think about every little possibility. It's only a matter of time before those fucking wasps realize that we're here. They're fast and strong and we're no match. Thing is, I'm not going to just sit here and wait for someone to come in here and save us. No one's coming. I know it. Not Matt, not anyone. We have to save ourselves."

Ollie sat there a moment, eyes trained on the openings that were indeed seeing less wasp traffic than before. He looked up to the wasps hanging on the ceiling, but he couldn't see the eyes close enough to observe whether they were watching he and Nikki and Shawna. "Okay," he said. "But we'll have to brace her."

Nikki nodded. "Of course. It's not like I want to leave anyone behind, but that we're in a survival situation, and not the kind that I can kick in the balls." Nikki stood. "If we get her standing and creep around the cave sticking to the back wall, it looks like we can make it to the openings pretty easy. At that point things will get kind of hairy, but I don't see any alternatives, do you?"

Ollie shook his head. He stood, Shawna's hand still held in his. "Can you get up?" he said to Shawna. She moved, but still lacked the mobility to raise herself from the cave floor. This time when she spoke, her voice came in a tender whisper. "Help. Me. I. Want to. Go."

Ollie and Nikki exchanged encouraging nods and helped Shawna up as gently as they could to avoid her making any sort of grunting noises that would attract the wasps. Nikki hefted Shawna's right side. "You're going to have to do your best to lift your feet so we don't drag them. Understand?"

Shawna nodded twice, slow and steadily.

"Great. Let's go."

With Shawna between them, Ollie and Nikki began the tedious task of walking in the deeply shadowed corners of the cave, both glancing at, but not making eye contact with the pile of bodies, all of which were docile and unmoving from the recent dosage of poison. Shawna lifted her feet, doing her best to match their slow, steady steps. Soon enough they were so interlocked that their breathing became tandem, as if they were subconsciously attempting to stifle their worrisome human noises for fear the big, bad wasps would swoop down and foil their plan of escape.

"Halfway there," said Nikki in but a whisper. "Need a break?"

Ollie shook his head, and, surprisingly, so did Shawna. At the shock on Ollie and Nikki's faces, Shawna offered a weak grin. If ever there were lingering doubts that what they were doing was right, that maybe they should have waited until Shawna was a hundred percent, that faint smile banished them. Ollie returned the smile and gave her a kiss that she was too weak to reciprocate. Her lips were chilled even in the desert heat that was caught in the cave, heat that was increasing as they approached the openings.

"Let's move," Nikki said.

They moved, and Shawna began to better assist, though she continued to rely on the help of her boyfriend and best friend like flesh-and-bone crutches. As they moved, Nikki frequently shifted her head around, watching the wasps on the ceiling. They too moved, slowly, always facing them, but not so much as fluttering their wings. Moonlight glinted off of their eerie black eyes like glistening drops of sap in the dark.

Ollie noticed Nikki's constant eyeing of the ceiling wasps. "What's up?"

"I think they're watching us. But it's weird, they're not doing anything about it."

"Maybe they don't know what we are."

"I don't know about that. They have a whole pile of people back there, and . . ." The words caught in Nikki's throat, choked off by the memory of seeing the larvae feeding in the nest. Was it worth telling Ollie what the bodies were for?

"Just so long as they don't come after us, I don't care what they do."

As they neared the openings they slowed, hyper cautious about their surroundings. A wasp flew into the opening further down the cave. It crawled across the floor on its human hands like something birthed of a nightmare, its human face twitching left and right, mandibles clacking. It zeroed in on the construction of a new nest, where several of the others were, depositing mud they had somehow managed to collect in the Mojave Desert.

"I'll have a look," said Nikki. She broke away from Ollie and Shawna, approaching the opening where the light of a million stars and a full moon seemed as brilliant as high noon after so much time in subterranean depths. She stepped out, felt the hot desert air like an oven awaiting a new batch of cookies, and that's when she said, "Oh shit."

The valley opened up, a picturesque expanse of dry brush and cacti out of a B-movie western, walled in by the very mountain Nikki had spent nearly twelve hours in. She looked out upon the brilliant vista, but more importantly she looked down, for she found herself at least two stories high. The only way down was a jagged mountainside of rock and sand that looked as precarious as walking a tight rope across the Grand Canyon.

"You've got to be kidding me." Ollie's voice came from behind.

"You didn't think it would be easy, did you?"

Another voice came from behind, a bit too eager, almost frantic: "Fresh air! Fresh air!"

Shawna stumbled forward, tripping over her own foot in her clumsy inability to fully control her limbs. Her body flung forward as if a projectile launched from a child's toy. She went over the edge face first. Ollie reached out for her, but it happened too fast. He had no chance to properly respond. In reaching for her, he moved forward and his shoe caught a thin layer of small rocks and dirt and his foot slid out from under him.

Shawna smacked boulders with her head as she plummeted down until her body lay still, tangled within a cluster of rocks, arms and legs akimbo, caked with blood and dust. Ollie, having the benefit of his facilities, managed to break his fall by turning around and landing on his chest. He reached out grabbing at something, anything, but there was nothing. The opening to the cave was smooth, having been traveled by the wasps over and over for months, maybe years.

Nikki moved to grab Ollie's hand, but she was too slow, perhaps too cautious, and he slipped away from her. He slid down the mountain, which aided in him not shattering his skull like Shawna had done, however he did take a nasty series of rolls, thwacking his arms and legs on rocks. His fate was to end up in a particularly nasty cluster of cacti that ended up in the scream heard 'round the Mojave Desert.

Chapter 18

Big Vic pulled the ice cream truck off the highway where Matt told him to do so. The tires didn't take the sand very well, which was disconcerting, considering they might have to make quite a getaway if these giant wasps were as much of a threat as Matt proclaimed them to be. Vic pressed the gas pedal harder, gaining enough speed to skim over the soft sand before the tires had a chance to dig in and get stuck, as they most certainly would if they were unable to find a good dry patch of desert floor to stop on.

The mountains rose before them, gaining in stature as they neared. "So this is the place?" Vic said.

Matt nodded, observing the mountains through the side window. "Pretty much. We'll have to get out and walk around. There's a opening, a sort of crevice that we have to walk through to get to the center of the mountains."

"Center?"

"Yeah, there's a valley in the middle."

"Sounds like a crater or something."

Walt had been quiet for most of the trip, sort of cowering in the corner, probably considering how this was all going to come down in the end. He had a lot to lose, what with his ice cream truck in the middle of the desert on some crazy mission against mutated wasps and enough dope to put him behind bars for a good stretch.

Matt trained his eyes on Walt, scowling at the poor sod. "Hey, what are you doing?"

Walt sat in an almost fetal position, head buried within his arms, between his legs. There was a prolonged snorting sound, and then he popped his head up, bloodshot eyes meeting Matt's.

"Better cut that shit out," Matt said.

Walt snorted back the drip in his throat. "You want my help in this bullshit rat-race you better let me get good and high. I'm no good all shaky and jonesing, man."

"We don't need you out of your fucking head either. I used to put enough of that shit up my nose to drop an elephant. I know how weird people get when they do too much." Matt eyed the freezer. "Looked like some real primo shit too."

Walt just stared with eyes like a bug, moving his mouth incessantly. It looked like he was chewing on imaginary food.

Big Vic pulled the ice cream truck up to the mountain, turning the wheel and making a wide circular u-turn, then positioning the truck to face the way they had come. He braked and cut the ignition. "I think we're on solid enough ground to get out of here." He turned around in his seat and focused on Walt. "You better not start up any of that weird tweaker shit. I'm serious. You think you gotta be high to do anything, maybe you're right. You've probably got so much of that shit in your blood you can't survive without it. But don't go off the fucking deep end, you hear?"

Walt's eyes darted this way and that. The speed hadn't merely crossed the blood brain barrier, but leapt over it. "Yeah, yeah, don't worry 'bout me." He snorted back another drip. "You don't want to see me without this stuff. I'm a mess."

Matt snickered. "Yeah you are. I've been there, bro. Meth just about fucked up my life, man." His voice lowered. "Better off without it."

Big Vic cut them off before words could escalate. "Let's get equipped. What do you got in here, Walt?"

As it turned out, Walt did indeed have a freezer full of ice creams, but pretty much lived out of his ice cream truck, thus there was quite a bizarre offering of potential supplies for their mission, the kind of stuff only a tweaker would possess, the most frightening of which was probably the guns.

Vic sighed. "What the fuck is wrong with you? You're selling ice cream to kids with a pile of drugs in the freezer and fucking guns? Christ, that's gotta be something like three felonies, maybe four." Vic was looking into the freezer that contained the meth. "How much dope is in here anyway? You trying to light up all of Laughlin with that?"

Walt smiled like a kid who had finally made it to the last level of an ornery video game. "I gotta friend who makes the shit. Right in his house. This stuff is pure as fuck. We got this agreement. He makes it; I sell it. No middle man, no one else selling this ultra pure ice in the tri-state area."

Vic tilted his head, as if pondering something. "Pure, huh? To me that translates to pretty fucking toxic. Gets your head all kinds of fucked up, right?"

Walt nodded. His eyes glittered with self-induced madness.

Matt had been quiet, just looking in at the dope. "Fuck, dude. That's blue ice, isn't it?"

Walt chuckled. "Damn straight. My buddy spent three years in Hawaii. Had to move back to the main land after some trouble with a manufacturer there, but he managed to copy the recipe."

Big Vic grunted. To think that his daughter was using this shit. "You got any backpacks, rucksacks, duffel bags, something like that."

Walt nodded. "Yeah, why?"

"We're gonna take this shit with us."

They loaded two backpacks and a cache bag with random items including a pair of hand-held gas welding torches, rope, lighter fluid, and the two guns.

"I'm not giving you one of my guns," Walt said to Big Vic.

"Like hell. You got my daughter into this shit, you're gonna hand over one of those pistols. Don't be a damn fool."

"Fuck, old man, you don't even know she's here."

"Yeah, well, until you can prove otherwise this is all I have to go on. I ain't gonna shoot you in the back or nothing, and when this is all said and done I'll give you your gun back. Think about it, it makes more sense to have two of us armed. It's not like I'm asking for both of your guns."

Walt considered this. He held out the gun and then pulled it back when Big Vic reached for it. "Hold up. You try anything funny I'm gonna shoot you dead, old man. Got it."

Big Vic struck his hand out quick like a ninja and grabbed the gun right out of Walt's hand. "That goes for the both of us."

Walt, visibly shaken and irritated by Vic's procurement of the firearm, started forward as if he was going to attempt retrieval of the weapon, but Big Vic stood his ground like a sturdy wall of man, unflinching, and this frightened Walt, who nodded and said, "Yeah, sure, let's go."

Vic's lip curled into a smirk of a crooked grin. Walt might have the guns because he was dealing large amounts of dope, but he was harmless. No one worth their salt would allow someone to just reach out and grab a gun away like that. Vic wondered how much of an asset he would be, all speeding on blue ice and too much of a pussy to pull the trigger or stand his ground. Matt, on the other hand, was fashioned from a different bolt of cloth. Vic figured he probably served in the military, though his reluctance to help his friends in distress kind of nixed that idea. Either way, he was probably more reliable than a tweaker.

They started walking, Matt leading the way. "This is fucked up. You guys both got guns. What do I have? A backpack full of random shit and this." Matt lifted the welding torch in one hand and a can of hairspray in the other. "By the time I get this torch lit I'll be slaughtered."

"You're on parole," Big Vic said. He cracked a rare grin. "You shouldn't be handling a gun."

"With that logic I shouldn't be running around with a couple of guys carrying, like, three pounds of speed. Shit, I bet the serial numbers are filed off those guns too."

"I'm a law abiding man," Vic said. "I had some rough and tumble years back in the day, but I've straightened out. I know Brandy went through quite a few years down a bad path, and I thought that I had helped her see the light. Not through Christ or anything like that. That's weak-minded bullshit. I just thought that having her away from her goddamned mother and being a good example of a human being helped." Big Vic took in a deep breath and let it out through his nose. "I was stupid to think I could save her. I love that girl to death, but maybe she was too far gone to begin with. Point is," he glanced at Matt, "I'll break fifty laws and commit a dozen felonies to get her back. One day you have a kid and you'll get it. Besides, your parole officer know you left the state?"

Matt didn't offer a response to that statement, which was just as good as a big fat "hell no", to which Vic's eyes twinkled with satisfaction, for he enjoyed having the last word.

They walked in silence for a while, Matt watching the sky for rogue wasps, until they made it to the crevice in the mountainside. Matt put his hands out, stopping them before entering the slender opening. He pointed upward. Perched on jutting rocks were two huge wasps. Their human faces were directed toward the approaching trio, black eyes staring like deep, glossy voids of nothing. The mandibles slowly pulsed as awkward mouths dripped a stream of goo like hungry dogs. They didn't so much as move.

"Do they see us?" Walt said in his loud version of a whisper.

"I don't know," Matt said, "but I painted houses for a summer and one of them had like a dozen wasp nests in the eaves. I noticed that there would be wasps working on the nest while two or three would sort of stand guard, just kind of hanging around watching for predators. Sometimes those ones would even go after us if we got too close."

"No shit?" Walt said.

"We'd just knock the nest down and swat the lingering wasps out of the air with a wide putty knife or piece of cardboard or something. Thing is, they would always come back. The next day there would always be a few that must have been out foraging for whatever they make their nests out of, and they would be right back where we knocked the previous nest down, just working hard to build another one. Territorial, I guess."

Big Vic held the gun in some kind of shooter's position, ready for action. "You think they'll just stay up there, or attack us as we walk through?"

"Fuck if I know, but I'm lighting this torch. Animals and bugs and shit don't like fire."

Matt set the hairspray down, pulled a lighter out of his pocket, and lit the torch, adjusting the blue flame to an easy orange wisp that flickered from the copper pipe jutting out of the hand-held gas tank. The flame danced in the black-orbed eyes of the sentinel wasps.

"Let's go," Big Vic urged.

They moved forward maybe four steps and then the wasps were on them. Their attack was so quick that, though they were anticipating a fight, everyone was caught off guard. One wasp headed for Vic. He let off a shot, but it went high.

The wasps grabbed him and lifted his body off the ground. He was about ten feet in the air when Walt's gun went off. The bullet hit Vic in the arm, traveled through his muscle and pierced the wasp. The many hands that clutched at Big Vic let go and he dropped. He hit the side of the mountain, which broke what would have been quite a fall for a man of his age. He rolled down and came to a stop in a fluff of crispy shrubbery. Big Vic moaned. He tried to move and screamed.

The other wasp, at that precise moment Vic was attacked, went for Matt, who, having dealt with the wasps before, was more prepared. He looked the thing straight in the eyes and blew a cloud of fire in its face by hitting the flame of his torch with a couple of blasts of hairspray. The wasp screamed something high in pitch that was human agony blended with the screech of an insect. The thing was approaching with such velocity that it slammed into Matt, face and arms aflame with burning hairspray. Matt twisted free from the burning mass and rolled around in the desert sand to get any lingering flames off of his body. The wasp writhed across the desert floor making abstract circles due to the damage its frantic fluttering wings sustained. It slowly burned to death and eventually lay in a heap of smoldering exoskeleton.

Matt rushed to Big Vic. Walt was already knelt beside him.

"I'm hurt bad," Vic said. "Got shot."

"Fuck," Walt said. "Sorry 'bout that, pops."

Big Vic coughed. He spoke between wheezing breaths. "Don't. You. Fucking. Call me that."

Matt offered a hand. "Can you move?"

Vic nodded, but waved Matt's hand away. "Yeah. I might. Pull through this. But not if those goddamned wasps come back. They find me here. They'll. Kill me. Something's broke. My leg. Maybe some ribs." He handed Matt the gun. "Take this. Find your friends, Matt. Find my Brandy."

Matt took the gun, nodded.

"Give me the backpack," said Walt. "Unless you think you could use the stuff inside."

"Didn't bring a first aid kit, did we?" Big Vic tried to laugh, but only choked. "Take the pack. You'll need more than I will."

Gritting his teeth, Big Vic leaned forward so that Walt could retrieve the backpack. He then leaned back against the side of the mountain, tilted his head toward the sky and took in several deep breaths.

"Come on, Walt," Matt said. "Let's get this shit over with."

"Just one thing," Walt said. He was still looking at Big Vic as if assessing the man. "Why did you insist we bring the meth?"

Vic took a moment to answer. "Shit's toxic." He paused, and then offered a wry smile. "Smoke 'em out."

Walt looked questioningly at Matt, who in turn shrugged and indicated that they should go, and so they did.

Chapter 19

Gretch gripped her service revolver tight, eyes scanning what she could see through the gaps in the pile of rocks she was hiding beneath with Sammy, who quietly lay there, paralyzed. "Did you hear that?"

He couldn't respond, but she had been talking to him the entire time, hours that seemed like some new form of mental torture, some sauna of deprivation that was teetering on heatstroke. Or maybe just minutes. Gretch had checked the time on Sammy's phone, but she was having a hard time remembering exactly when they arrived to the canyon. Once things went sideways she kind of lost track of time altogether.

Face a glossy sheen of sweat, uniform sticking to her body, Gretch decided that she couldn't sit there beneath the rocks any longer. Those things that attacked, those mutated wasps with their human faces caused a deeper fear within Gretch than she had experienced in all her life. She had dealt with guns being drawn on her, taking down men twice her size who were loaded on angel dust, dead bodies that had been rotting in hundred degree weather, but the wasps were something she never could have prepared for. They were the type of thing that was reserved for shitty drive-in movies and bad novels. The kind of thing a jaded artist paints in the wake of a fever dream. Not reality. And that was something she had great difficulty dealing with. How the hell was she supposed to handle these things?

It took a lot of courage to even accept the fact that she was going to have to face those fears else she dehydrate or go insane. Sammy was alive, but completely paralyzed and she felt horribly for him. Would he ever walk again? Had the stinger damaged his spinal column? Would he make it out of the rocks, the desert? Not if she didn't do something.

The gunshot—for Gretch was certain that's what she heard—brought her focus back full throttle, away from the fears of giant wasps. A gunshot was something she understood. A gunshot was something she could deal with. A gunshot meant that perhaps her phone call to the sheriff's station had gone through and reinforcements were looking for her.

"Look," she said to Sammy. His eyes just stared, but she could see that he heard. "I'm going to go out for help. I think help's out there. I won't forget you, you hear me? I will come back, I swear."

He didn't move, but she could see in his eyes that he believed. Or at least she told herself that. He blinked more readily, so there was that.

Gretch turned, lay flat on her belly, and slinked her way through the narrow opening from which she and Sammy had gotten into the rock barrier. During her training she had to go through an obstacle course with walls to climb, hurdles to jump, and even some crawling through tight tunnels, very similar but not nearly as rigorous as boot camp training. Never, at the time, had she thought she would actually have to crawl the way they had taught her. It had seemed like such a useless lesson at the time. Even now that she was doing that very crawl, it felt more instinctual. Crawling was crawling, especially when fear was a motivator.

The air was no less stifling outside of the rock cluster. Typical Mojave Desert summer night. The stars shined like millions of glassy freckles on a massive black void, with the moon nearly full shining like a beacon. Rocks created shadows that could conceal anything, but Gretch wasn't worried about the sidewinder or the scorpion. They were minor nuisances compared to giant wasps with human faces and hands. God, those hands. They had grabbed her. Even now Gretch could feel those many fingers digging into her legs, ripping at her pants.

What happened to Florence?

Everything happened so quickly when the wasps attacked. She remembered her partner getting jabbed with a stinger and then being carried away. The memory of what happened, though it was only hours ago, seemed impossible. Like some hallucination. How could there be insects the size of human beings flying around, and how is it she had never seen one before? How long has this secret dwelled in the mountains unknown?

A glint caught Gretch's eyes. It was Deputy Florence's pistol lying on the sun-baked ground, moonlight reflecting off the polished chrome. He had dropped it when the wasp took him away. From the pistol, Gretch's eyes scanned the horizon, rising up the mountain and stopping at the cave openings, the ones she had been watching with her binoculars.

Holstering her revolver, Gretch pulled her compact binoculars for a better view. She'd watched wasps come and go from within the rocks, flying in lazily and making jettisoned getaways. She realized just then how much safer she felt in the rocks, however hot and sweaty those close confines were. Now, in the open, there was a whole new sense of dread, as if anything could happen, and where did bizarre insect mutations end? If giant wasps were a thing, then what about spiders and scorpions and honeybees?

Gretch's focus was steady, zeroed in on one of the many

caves on the side of the mountain, the one, she thought, that she had been watching before. Suddenly, a wasp shot out of the opening. As if assaulted, Gretch yelped and stumbled backwards, almost falling on the ground. She dropped the binoculars and pulled her gun, training a bead on the thing and following it through the air. Remembering her training, she aimed ahead of her target and let off three consecutive shots.

The second bullet hit the wasp. It's wings fluttered irregularly and then it went into something close to a barrel roll with a diagonal trajectory aiming for the desert floor. On its way down, the thing let out a wailing cry that was so human in nature Gretch sucked in a breath and held it, as if, for just a second, she thought of the beast as human.

It hit the desert floor in a flurry of dust, rolling hard, arms tearing from the abdomen and launching through the air like fleshy projectiles. Another human touch to this monstrosity that threatened a gag reflex, but Gretch managed to hold it back. They don't prepare you to see these sorts of things in the academy. At this point she would gladly go back to that horrible day last summer when she was the sole officer doing a welfare check. She smelled the body before seeing it, and that was an image she had nightmares about for two straight weeks. Gretch wasn't the type of officer who felt the necessity of therapy concerning the traumas of what she did for a living, but walking into that bedroom where the poor bastard blew his brains out and seeing the layer of decomposition that saturated the wood floor beneath the body was something her mind struggled with. Right about now she would go back there and deal with the dead rather than these things.

The strained, whiny cry that was sung from the dying wasp as it descended acted as a warning signal or perhaps a plea for help. Three more wasps shot out of the cave, one after the other. They all zeroed in on their fallen brethren, landing beside the wrecked corpse. Silently, Gretch watched them crawl around on human hands, much the way a tiny little wasp would, circling the dead and tilting their human heads like curious dogs. They picked up the dismembered arms and examined them with glassy onyx eyes, sniffed them, and finally licked with tongues thin and long that darted from their mouths like proboscises.

This time Gretch couldn't hold back the urge to puke. Try as she might, it happened all at once in a reflex so strong the vomit sprayed from her mouth, the sound of which drew the attention of the three wasps. They dropped the limbs they were dutifully checking and swarmed her.

Without even wiping her face, Gretch lifted her gun and drew a bead on one of the approaching wasps. She pulled off a shot and hit the thing right in the head. It ate dust, but the other two were on her quicker than she could take aim. She let off as many shots as she could, but they went wild. She turned and ran back toward the cluster of rocks where Sammy waited, unmoving.

***

Sammy could hear more than he could see what was going on, and he was in no position to move. The wasp had paralyzed him. He figured the poison was strong, perhaps intensified in their mutated form. With his eyes he had urged Gretch to go, hoping that she could get help, but he really didn't know what the point was. What would it be like living as a vegetable? He couldn't even commit suicide if he wanted to.

After Gretch left the rocks Sammy was alone with his thoughts. She had been talking to him a lot, which turned out to be more frustrating than comforting, though he understood that she was talking for both his sake and for the sake of her sanity. The life of a veggie-case? No thanks. Sammy was mildly relieved to see her go, not only for the possibility of getting help, but for the alone time as well. He had always harbored resentment toward the police. He felt that they treated him differently because of his dark complexion, but right now he had everything riding on this one, and he liked to believe that she would, indeed, come back for him.

Gunfire jolted him, actually causing his body to shake and tremble. Did people who had become paralyzed experience that sort of thing? Involuntary trembling from trauma? More gunshots and a scream. *Gretch!*

Unable to switch to a better vantage or even move his head so that he could see better, Sammy watched as best he could through the seams in the rocks. The brilliant moon was doing a decent job at illuminating the desert night. Gretch was running, Sammy could hear her footfalls, the sound rising. She was coming back, but not with help.

Then something happened.

Gretch tripped and fell. Through the rocks Sammy could see her hit the desert floor hard, an exasperated grunt firing from deep within her throat. The wind was knocked out of her. Her sweaty face was covered in a layer of fresh dust that made her look kind of like someone at a tribal ceremony. She opened her eyes, bright white against the fresh dirt that settled on her sweat-slicked skin. Their eyes connected, wide and agonized and then the two wasps were on her. Gretch had no chance.

Sammy was forced to watch for he couldn't control his eyes enough to close them at will. The wasps savaged her with stings, very unlike the one sting he was given. They thrust the black swords from the ass-end of their abdomen over and over, filling her with holes until she went limp. Once she was lifeless, they used their human hands and removed her clothes, ripping and yanking the garments, clearly unfamiliar with the concept of buttons and zippers. Savage. Brutal. Once she was naked and bleeding they went at her with their mandibles, ripping and tearing at the soft spots, eviscerating her, shredding her muscles, tearing her face.

They reduced Gretch to a pile of bleeding flesh, torn tubes of intestine sprouting from her exposed guts, and then they rolled her body in the sand, coating the fresh corpse. Sammy wanted to yell, to scream, to cry, to do something, but he was unable. His body trembled, his brain ached. If he were to make it out of this situation he would not be the same man. If he managed to regain his bodily function, he would still be broken.

Gretch's blood seeped through the layer of sand, and then the wasps rolled her across the desert floor again. They did this a few times until her body was nothing more than a bulky shape coated with a cocoon of tightly packed, blood-wet sand, and then they both grabbed her and flew in tandem. Escaping Sammy's vantage, they carried the body through the air and into the cave.

CHAPTER 20

THE GUNSHOTS PUT FIRE UNDER WALT AND MATT'S FEET. THEY navigated their way through the slender crevice, hopping shrubs and cactus and dodging rocks, whose sole purpose it seemed, at that very moment, was to trip them up. When the crevice opened to the strange little valley walled in on all sides by mountains, they stopped at the sound of movement rustling the sand. Down yonder they saw the wasp duo rolling something across the desert floor.

Matt whispered, "Is that a body?"

Walt shook his head. "Fuck if I know."

The wasps lifted the shape and flew to one of the cave openings in the side of the mountain. The night was again still, lit generously by the moon and stars, but dim enough to create a multitude of shadows. When giant wasps were the cause for discontent, the idea of some smaller, more human fear hiding within the shadows seemed childish.

Matt's eyes were fixed on the cave the wasp had gone through. "That's where we need to go."

"Follow that giant fucking wasp? You crazy? There's gotta be a ton of them up in there. They'd rip us apart in no time."

"Then what are we doing here, you and me? If that's the

way you feel about it we might as well turn back. Jump in your ice cream truck and high tail it back to Needles. Who cares, right? We can just leave this little secret to the desert sands."

Walt didn't say anything. He looked nervous, twitching and scratching.

Matt looked at Walt like the tweaker truly disgusted him. "We'll have to pass by Big Vic, of course, you know, on the way out. If he's still alive he's going to wonder how things went. What are you going to tell him? You going to make some shit up about looking for his daughter? I mean, it's not like he's going to come after you, even if I tell him what kind of pussy you are, that you turned like a yellow-bellied prick and ran away."

Walt was becoming increasingly irritated. He pulled a small baggie from his pocket. Matt made a gesture to stop him, and then thought better of it. Walt had a serious case of meth jitters. At this point, he needed that stuff. He would be useless without it. In some psychotic sense of reason, the meth would focus him, just so long as he didn't over do it, but there was no way for Matt to judge how much he'd taken and how much he could abuse without completely losing his mind. Poor bastard had to do *some*thing to stifle the ticks. He was starting to look like he had Tourette's.

After a pinch of crystal up each nostril, Walt said, "Alright, fuck it. I'm no hero, man. I don't even know what I'm doing here." His eyes were bloodshot and looked like party favors that would explode from his face if someone pulled on the optic nerve. "Things is, even though Big Vic believes that I didn't do anything to Brandy, I mean, anything to do with her disappearance, I still think he has this idea I *did* do something to her. Look, man, truth is I really cared about Brandy. I fucked up. I pissed her off and she ran away. That's it. It's not like I think I have some future with her, but if she's here somewhere I'd like to find her."

"I'll tell you what, if it wasn't for that girl coming out of nowhere I wouldn't be out here. It made no sense. Something's going on here. Something that has to do with missing people and those giant wasps. Just before leaving the sheriff's station I noticed a bulletin board with a lot of missing persons on it. Way too many for a little shitheel town like Needles. I mean, maybe some of them were from Laughlin, but even then it seemed excessive." Matt shifted his gaze back to the mountain, to the caves. "Because of that woman we brought into town—"

"Delanie."

Matt nodded. "You know she was missing?"

Walt shook his head. "Dude, I'm out of the loop on things like current events 'n' shit. I had no idea so many people were missing. A lot of people left suddenly, but that's not all that unusual in a place like Needles. I've been thinking about leaving. Straightening my life out. It's hard to get out, you know."

Matt nodded and raised an eyebrow. "Yeah, sure, that explains the life supply of dope in your backpack. Can't get out if you can't stop that shit."

Walt grunted. "Look, it's not as easy as it sounds. It's so hard to get out of this life. I've tried. It just . . . it just pulls you back in, man."

Matt nodded with recognition of Walt's plight. "I get it, really I do. Prison straightened me out. Kind of a shitty way to have to deal with one's problems though. You should really try—"

Two wasps, holding something in their hands, flew out of the cave, distracting Matt from what might have turned into a cautionary monologue. The wasps glided slowly to the canyon floor. Darkness concealed the contents of their hands, abstract parcels that they dropped on the sand, rolling them around until the sand clung to the items, doubling them in size. Clutching their possessions, the wasps took flight and returned to the cave.

"What the hell was that all about?" Walt said.

"I don't have clue. I just know that we have to get up there."

"Maybe we should go through one of these other caves. They probably all meet up—"

"No. It's like a maze in there. That's how my friends got lost. I can't even know for sure they're up there. Might be lost within the mountain. If that's the case, we'll never find them. You good at rock climbing?"

Walt looked at Matt like he was crazy. "Rock climbing?"

"Doesn't look that hard. Hey, before we go up there, I want to do something. Let me see that backpack."

Walt snickered. "You sure. It's got the dope in it. You've been doing everything you can to avoid this shit, like your parole officer's gonna come out from behind a cactus and bust you."

"I fucking hate that shit, that's all. I'd rather not have to even look at the stuff. Look, lets fill that backpack with some of this dry grass and shit. Anything dry. Just pack it in there, as much as we can fit."

"What the hell for."

Matt shrugged. "A long shot."

After filling the backpack fit to burst with dry grass and brush, they cautiously approached the mountainside of caves. Matt had taken notice of a particularly ragged rock jutting from the cave he'd been focused on, the one the wasps had gone into. That was the only way to differentiate one cave from the other.

"The fuck . . .?" Walt knelt down and picked up a gun.

"Probably from one of the cops," Matt said. "Take it. We can use all the help we can get."

They trudged along until they were gazing upon the threatening mountainside towering above. Rocks protruded at random, leading a path as yet unknown. Something leaning against a boulder caught Matt's attention. Carefully he climbed up the side of the mountain to have a look. It was a body.

It was Shawna's body.

"Awww man." Matt slumped and looked away.

Walt hadn't begun the climb yet. He looked at Matt with worried eyes. "What is it?"

Matt shook his head slowly as if unable to process the dead girl. "Shawna. A friend."

"Shit."

There was no use even trying for a pulse. Shawna's head was pulped into the rock that had broken her fall. The brains and blood were already coagulating in the dry heat of the desert night with sporadic skull fragments like corn kernels in shit.

"We've still got to go up there," Matt said. "There are others. Maybe they're still alive."

After taking a moment to scout a path, Matt began his ascent. Walt followed closely behind, navigating the slick, sand-covered rock like he'd done this before. Halfway up they ran into someone else.

Matt squinted. "Ollie?"

Ollie stood leaned up against a large boulder. He was unrecognizable due to the layers of dust and sand coating his sweat-slick face and arms that caused him to look a bit like a coal miner after a hard day underground. He bore many cuts sealed over with dried blood and had a look in his eyes like he'd gazed upon Father Death and lived to tell the tale.

"I gotta get out of here," Ollie said. It was as if he didn't even recognize Matt. "We all gotta get out of here."

Matt shifted to allow Walt room on the side of the mountain. "Were you up there, in the cave?"

Ollie nodded. "Nikki. She's still up there. I . . . I was trying to . . . to save Shawna . . . but—"

Matt looked away. He knew how much Ollie loved Shawna. He figured Ollie was going to be the first to settle down. Matt always messed with him and said he'd be the first of them to pop the question and fuck up his life. Matt even jokingly offered him a jar with Shawna's name on it to keep his balls in.

Ollie's eyes dribbled tears that ran dark lines on his sand-caked face. "I tried, Matt. I had her."

"It's all right," Matt said. He patted Ollie's shoulder, which was about as much emotional consolation as he was capable of considering his incredible machismo attitude and the adrenaline that was currently flowing through his veins. Walt held back in silence, watching the sky and the caves for troublesome wasps. Matt continued, "Well, if Nikki is up there, we've got to try and get her. You seen Sammy? I lost track of him outside when the wasps attacked."

"You've seen the wasps too?"

"Fuck yes! They chased me out of here. Actually chased the sheriff's car. I ran into this guy and some other dude who thinks his daughter is in here. I have no idea what to expect, but we have to at least try to get in there and . . . fuck, I don't know. Why don't you make your way down the mountain? Can you do that?"

Ollie nodded. "I think. I might have broken some ribs or something, but I've been trying to get down. Slow but steady."

"Whatever you do, don't look at Shawna. Seriously. Just avoid looking at her."

Ollie nodded. His eyes welled.

"And if you have your phone try for a signal. Call 911. Call someone, anyone."

Ollie nodded again. "There's a lot of them up there."

"Wasps?" Matt said. "Yeah, I was afraid of that."

Ollie shook his head. "No. I mean people. Bodies."

Matt exchanged a shocked glance with Walt, who, despite being loaded on speed, looked terrified. "Bodies?"

Ollie nodded. "The wasps sting them, but they don't kill

them. The people are poisoned. They can't move. Piled like wood. Some are dead."

Two wasps zipped out of the cave. Everyone looked up as they flew over. Walt flinched and ducked into a squatting position. Like the previous pair of wasps, they were holding something. A drip fell from the sky as they passed, hitting Walt smack in the center of his head. He jerked backward so violently that he almost lost his footing and went the way of Shawna. After regaining his balance, he wiped the wetness from his forehead only to see a red slick across the back of his hand. He smelled it. "Oh, fuck, gross. It's blood!"

Again, the wasps descended into the valley, dropped their load and rolled the bloody objects in the sand until packed with dirt. They ascended and flew back into the cave, not even noticing the humans on the side of the mountain.

"This is fucking crazy," Matt said. "Have a snort if you need it, Walt, 'cause it's time to see just what in the fuck we're dealing with."

CHAPTER 21

Nikki stood just inside the cave, out of the wasp's sight, contemplating what to do when she saw Matt and the skinny guy with the terribly pockmarked face standing near Shawna's body. Nikki couldn't see exactly what shape Shawna was in, but she could tell that her friend wasn't moving.

Nikki tucked herself back into a shadow and watched as the wasps worked their grisly construction of the new nest. She watched as one would pull a dead body from the bottom of the pile, sometimes so rotten it would tear in half, blackened guts trailing the torso as it was pulled to the center of the cave. With gusts created from so many frantic wings, putrid odors attacked Nikki's nostrils. She puked in her mouth a few times, but managed not to make any noises that would arouse the wasps' attention. They took the bodies and yanked off the limbs like pulling a drumstick off a Thanksgiving turkey. Popped the head off with a twist and a snap of the spine. The parts were ripped and torn into wet hunks of cannibal chum, all glistening and stinking of decay. Then each wasp would grab a sticky body part and fly out of the cave. When they returned, the body parts were three or four times their size, coated in a thick paste of desert sand, tightly packed and soaked in decomposition juices and sticky, rotting flesh. The parts would then be deposited near the new nest where another team of wasps began stripping the rot-mud and packing the stuff like wet adobe.

Nikki sat in her corner watching this play out, over and over. She wanted to move, but the mechanical movements of the wasps had pulled her into some kind of trance. Maybe she could sit here and nap through this, wait for the first rays of the morning sun and slip out like an innocent lizard or rattler.

And then she remembered that Matt was coming. Matt. She didn't know him all that well, being that he and Sammy were Ollie's friends. She'd met him at least once before at a club. He was cocky and that turned her off. She liked nice guys and found the overly-confident to be more asshole than charm, though she could swear most girls fell for that shit. Now, sitting in a dusty cave that smelled awfully of the dead, Nikki hoped that macho bullshit attitude was in full force. If the guy looked in the mirror and saw Chuck Norris and Steve McQueen, The Rock and Schwarzeneggar, all the better. That didn't make the guy smart, and surely, in Nikki's mind, not attractive, but maybe there was such a thing as dumb luck.

Matt and Walt climbed the mountain, each foothold a cautious effort. Wasps shot out of the opening they were heading for in random intervals, causing the guys to crouch and remain still each time. The wasps seemed to be more concerned with the bloody bundles they were rolling in the sand than anything else.

Just before reaching the cave, Walt said, "What the hell are we getting into?" he was pouring sweat.

Matt glanced at Walt and his eyes were brimmed with fear, but he wouldn't dare acknowledge that. Shawna was dead, Ollie was half crazed and wandering the desert. He had no idea where Sammy was. Had he gone into one of the caves? And then there was that Nikki girl. She was Shawna's friend. She had stayed behind with Ollie to look for Shawna. Ollie said she was in the cave. Why hadn't she come out?

"We're saving lives." Matt's voice was dreamy. Images lingered in his mind. Images of Shawna's head splattered on the rocks, images of him leading them into this mountain canyon. His military service did not lead him into battle, did not lead him to witness the horrors of war. None of his friends knew it, but he was honorably discharged. The reason he never told anyone was that he was ashamed, because the truth was he couldn't take it. He was too much of a hot head and too insecure. He found a loophole, realized that it was easy to be discharged if you spent time with a psychologist and said the right things.

Matt snapped out of his headspace. Thoughts of his biggest disgrace haunted him from time to time, but he never let on about it. He had to cut out the self-pity and get in the game. This stupid excursion was his idea, after all. How could he just abandon even one of his friends when he was the one that led them to this doom?

They made it to the cave opening and stepped inside. The expanse of the cave was shrouded in darkness that their eyes had trouble adjusting too considering how bright the moonlight was outside. Matt squinted and ducked as if a wasp would swoop down and deliver him to his maker. The buzzing intensified with every step they took.

"Matt?"

Matt's ears perked up at the sound of a woman's voice, but he was still having a hard time seeing in the dark. "Nikki?"

Blinking his eyes over and over, Matt slowly shuffled toward the voice, and that's when he was embraced. The hug came out of nowhere and almost knocked him down since he wasn't expecting it.

Through tears, Nikki said, "You came back."

Buzzing grew loud and they could feel the gust of rushed air as a pair of wasps swooped by them. Matt and Nikki collapsed to the ground in fear of being spotted. In a sharp whisper she said, "This way! In the corners."

"I can't see shit," Matt said, searching frantically with his hands like someone who had dropped their prescription eyeglasses.

"Just keep still. They haven't noticed me yet."

Walt followed Matt and Nikki to the corner of the cave. He blinked his eyes repeatedly as they adjusted. Sweat spread in arcs from his armpits and matted his shirt to his back. As if whispering to himself he said, "Those fucking stingers, man."

Nikki's gleaming eyes flashed toward Walt. "The poison incapacitates fully."

Walt's brow wrinkled. Nikki took that gesture to mean that he didn't understand what she said. "The poison paralyzes people. Temporarily. When I found—" She trailed off and looked away. Her eyes became shiny with developing tears. "I was stung. But I managed to get over the paralysis. Shawna didn't fare so well. She was . . . she was still dazed when she fell over the edge." Nikki shook her head slowly, as if contemplating recent events. "There wasn't much we could do."

Matt put his hand on Nikki's shoulder. She was hesitant, averting her eyes. She didn't know Matt well enough to have him see her cry, and though she had been through a lot, she felt that allowing his offer of the close comfort that good friends and loved ones shared would do nothing to help. She put her hand on his, gently squeezed it and said, "We have to get out of here." That's when something dawned on her. Sadness evacuated her eyes, temporarily at least. "What are you doing here? Did you actually come back for us? Did you bring help?"

"Tried. Wasps got 'em. That was the first time I came back.

I drove a police SUV back to Needles and ran into this guy—" he gestured toward Walt "—and an old man. We all got ambushed. The old man's holed up, but hurt. He—" Matt shot a questioning look to Walt. "It's his daughter, right?"

Walt nodded. "Brandy. She went missing. Pops thinks she's here."

Nikki raised her eyes and slowly pivoted her head in a way that invited both Matt and Walt to follow her gaze. "There are a lot of people in here. Some alive. Probably more dead. Over there. Piled up. Poisoned." Her focus shifted toward a huge structure of dried mud built off of the far wall of the cave. From this distance it was clear that they were looking at a massive mud wasp nest. "Others are in there."

Matt shook his head. "Jesus."

They all stood there in silence, the gravity of the situation seeping in and taking hold. Questions of survival and heroics lingered in the air as if discussed in some weird manner of ESP.

Nikki spoke up. "I told them that I would come back, that I would try to get them out." Any previous hope had been vanquished from her voice as if the fate of so many people was a foregone conclusion.

Matt nodded, staring at the wasps working on the new nest. The ones on the ceiling watched the three of them, those glassy onyx eyes staring like sentinel security cameras. "We came in here looking for you and Shawna and Ollie, but also Brandy. Right, Walt?"

Walt nodded, hesitantly at first. "Yeah. I owe it to the old man. And I'd like to clear my name."

"So how do we save everybody?" Matt said. "Is that even possible?"

Nikki swallowed hard. "I don't think we can. They're completely paralyzed. Even if we managed to get them over to the cave opening, they would fall like Shawna. And I don't know that we could do much without attracting attention.

That happened, you know. One of those wasps came down and jabbed its stinger into the pile, just stabbing people at random until the poor bastard who was moaning shut the fuck up. Just kept stabbing. Killed people. They want some of them alive, believe me, but they're savage. Not a lot of brains in those human heads. Just big scary-ass bugs."

Matt shook his head and shifted his weight into a more comfortable position. "I don't know. Is it worth it, trying to save them right now? Maybe we need to get out of here and get help. Real help. A situation like this needs the National fucking Guard."

Walt had been quiet for a guy whose mind was spinning. He found himself in a deeply retrospective mood, helped along by the strain of their current position and the darkness of the cave. "I want to find Brandy. I've *got* to find Brandy."

Nikki nodded. "Look, there's no way we save everyone, but if we can find Brandy, maybe we can get her out of here. Her dad's outside?"

Walt nodded. "Yeah."

"Then I don't want to have to face him without his daughter, or at least some kind of closure. I mean, a lot of the people, they're dead." She shook her head, exasperated, and sighed. "I kind of agree with Matt. This is a way bigger problem than we can handle."

Matt pulled out his cell phone. "You know what, I'm gonna take a picture of the wasps. People need to know about this. It's just too crazy. We go to the Bullhead City PD or Laughlin or whatever and they're going to laugh at us."

Matt lifted his phone and swiped the screen, bringing a glow of blue light across his face that changed into a dark rectangle. He tapped the little lightning bolt that turned on the flash, illuminating the cave in a tiny light that seemed to be amplified.

Nikki moved to grab the phone. "Shit, Matt, don't do that!"

But it was too late. He snapped the picture, an obnoxious little sound like an old fashioned camera issued way too loud in the cave. The flash of light threw the wasps into a panic.

"Dammit, Matt. What the hell did you do that for?"

Matt pocketed his phone and the wasps took flight, converging on the area where Matt, Nikki and Walt sat huddled against a crook in the cave wall. Fearful of what would happen were they to become cornered, they all fled in different directions.

Matt headed toward the cave openings (he seemed to have more flight than fight when it came to adversaries that were bigger than him, just like his service in the military), while Nikki stuck to the shadows, heading toward the body pile.

Walt, he ran across the center of the cave, headed straight for the massive mud nest.

Chapter 22

When the menial flash of Matt's phone disrupted the wasps all hell broke loose. The attack was so sudden and unexpected that everyone hoofed it in three different directions.

Walt didn't think strategy. His attention had been on the mud nest. He'd seen them before, caked on the stucco of the apartment building he grew up in. He'd never thought those kind of wasp nests were nearly as interesting as the paper wasp nests, and in the presence of a mud nest that was human sized, he'd found himself transfixed. It was a good focal point, which was something anyone with a head full of blue meth needed. It felt as if the blood in his veins was pumping faster than normal, a feeling Walt knew well and even embraced, but here in this dark cave with monstrous insects at the ready he felt trapped in his own skin. It was a feeling he despised, one that brought on deep, dark inner thought, the worst of which was that Brandy was here somewhere, and in some capacity he was at fault. That night she went missing he had been out of his mind. He thought she was just as fucked off as he was, but it turned out she wanted to break up with him. She said that she needed space to clear her head. Said she didn't like the woman she was becoming, didn't want to go down that well-trodden path she walked when she was a teenager. She was going to go back to her daddy and ask for forgiveness, ask him to help her kick the drugs, check into rehab, whatever it took. In addition to being his girlfriend, Brandy had become Walt's drug buddy. He felt that connection between them was strong, and he didn't take to her rejection of him and his way of life very nicely. He became aggressive, and then she was out of the car. Into the night. Gone.

Walt ran straight toward the mud nest. Not the new one being constructed, but the older one tucked into a corner on the other side of the cave near the pile of bodies Nikki had pointed out earlier. There were openings in the mud nest to hide in and the wasps seemed to be more focused on the construction of the new one. Perhaps the old nest was vacant of wasps.

And Nikki said there were people in there.

If the bodies lying atop the pile were dead, perhaps those within the mud nest were alive.

In his sprint, Walt didn't see what happened to the others. He ran as fast as he could and reached the nest quickly. From behind a static buzzing assaulted his ears and he turned just in time to see a wasp approaching. The face of the beast was stoic, eyes glossy and reflecting the moonlight that spilled into the cave from the openings in the mountain. Walt slipped into the mud nest, the opening small, but easy for his slender frame to crawl inside. It was tight and dark, but he fumbled his way backward. The wasp's bulk filled the opening, but all it could do was look inside. It was a big one, perhaps the biggest Walt had seen, or maybe it was bigger than life up close. Either way, it couldn't get inside. It just stared, mandibles clacking together in rigid snaps fit to dismember human bodies.

In his rush to retreat, Walt pushed his way into something

gooey, palming a pile of soft muck that his hand sunk into. He pulled his hand free and released some kind of retched odor that caused him to vomit. After puking, he spit several times to get the taste of bile out of his mouth. He was so parched that he began to feel weak. Walt needed water.

And then he heard a sound from behind, within the nest.

Nikki ran back to familiar ground. A few hours ago she'd awoken on the body pile, and there she returned, only this time she grabbed a body from the top (a man with a saliva-slick beard who may or may not be deceased), and pulled him down. He slid off the pile like so much dead weight. Nikki jumped back to avoid getting crushed beneath his girth. She used his body as a shield and lay in wait. If a wasp came down to jab new doses of poison into the unfortunates in the human pile, she might be spared. If she were to get stung again, she could always try her mind tricks, but she wasn't about to depend on that.

Lying there she wondered how she found herself back where she started. Why hadn't she gone out of the cave? What were she and the other two going to accomplish against a hive of mutated wasps? They were goddamned stupid to think they could save anyone.

She'd been at the mouth of the cave. She'd felt the warm air from outside.

Now she wallowed in rotting flesh and listless people waiting like living slabs of beef.

Matt ran toward the cave openings, but he passed them by, too afraid that the wasps would see him in the moonlight and either collect him for their midnight pleasure or push him over the edge. Instead, he found some rocks to crouch behind. They weren't very big, not enough to conceal him.

Matt pulled the pistol and aimed toward the incoming wasps. He pulled off a few shots, but his aim was for shit. The sound of the gun, however, startled the flying beasts, and they zipped off in varying directions. Matt took this opportunity to arm himself with a couple of baseball-sized rocks. When the first of the three that were swooping in on him returned, he waited until it was close enough and threw the rock at its head. The years he played baseball helped his aim and the rock pegged the fleshy human face, tearing one of the little black eyes off. The wasp made a hard turn as if to get away and ended up going head-first into the side of the cave close to one of the two openings. The head was obliterated on impact. The body collapsed to the ground in a sickening heap. Arms stretched in all directions, twitching and moving from the last vestiges of its dying nervous system. The abdomen ruptured when the thing hit the cave floor. A substance like bloody pus with the texture of cottage cheese leaked from the wound as if under pressure.

The wasps were agitated, but they held back for the moment. Matt just leaned against the cave wall and watched, ready to pitch a rock if he had to, though he was sure he couldn't repeat what he had just done. That was once in a life-time kind of stuff. Given a hundred chances he probably couldn't bean another one of those things right in the face, and that worried him.

Matt pulled off his backpack, careful not to make much noise. From within he drew some of the contents. In his hand was one of those little green Coleman propane canisters, the type that was typically used for a lantern, or for manufac-turing meth in an ice cream truck.

At this point, Matt wasn't even entertaining the idea of saving any one. If he, Nikki and Walt could get out that was the best-case scenario. *The others are dead anyway.* Matt told himself that. He had to, because he had a plan, and they had to be dead.

Matt nodded his head and shook the propane cylinder in his grip as if judging the weight of the thing. *Yeah, those bodies over there are dead, just piled up like firewood.*

CHAPTER 23

Nikki heard the gunshots and flinched, the sound echoing through the cave in a way that made it hard to pinpoint where they came from. There were no sounds of buzzing wasp wings close by, but she remained in concealment for another few minutes after the gunshots subsided before slowly emerging from behind the body of the bearded man. While they lay there playing possum she could feel his stomach gently rise and lower. It was an eerie feeling, like a corpse come back to life, and she suddenly felt guilty about using him as a living shield.

Nikki crouched down behind the pile of suffering humans, popping her head up just enough to see the cave, but it was dark. The moon made its way over the mountain and soon they would be without light, a thought that terrified Nikki to no end. But, as scared as she was, she couldn't leave the other two behind. *What about the bearded man? What about the others on the pile, the ones who haven't died yet?*

Nikki had been unconsciously avoiding eye contact with any of the people lying atop the mount of cordwood humans. She didn't want to see their pleading eyes because she knew there was nothing she could do to help them, and it hurt to see them staring, terrified, conscious of their dire predicament but unable to do a damn thing about it.

Looking across the darkening cave she couldn't see who had fired the gun. She wasn't sure where Matt and Walt had run, but she had the impression that they fled in different directions.

Oh how Nikki wished she had a gun right about now. Her father had taught her how to shoot clay pigeons and empty beer cans, but she didn't own a gun. Living in an apartment with roommates it seemed like a bad idea to have a firearm in the house, and even if she did have one she wouldn't have brought it with her on a trip to Lake Havasu. Right about now a gun seemed like the best defense.

The wasps appeared to have been startled by the sound of gunfire. They were agitated, spinning in tight circles in the middle of the cave at rapid speeds. Some of them clung to the ceiling, crawling in zigzag patterns. Nikki watched, waiting for the right moment to make a move.

The mud nest smelled of old pennies and human foulness, but Walt, who had lived in squalor for many years of his life, wasn't affected by such smells the way most other people were. What grated on him were the sounds, the slurping and suckling, the dripping on the floor and powerful whiffs of blood. The blood smells choked him up. He hated blood. He'd never shot dope because of the blood that entered the needle before being plunged into the veins of the user. Blood made him squeamish.

And he knew the rich coppery odor was that of blood. He suspected that what he heard dripping onto the floor was the same.

Walt pulled the phone, fumbling it in his shaking hands. He turned it on(noting that he had no service), and directed the screen forward to see what he was dealing with. That's when his stomach dropped. Throughout the tight concaves woven in the blood-mud there were at least a dozen forms. They looked like giant maggots with human baby faces all chubby and nightmarish. The organs and veins were visible through translucent skin. Their little bulbous eyes were cataract, blind, but they must have sensed the light, a light that, though tiny from the screen of a phone, illuminated the mud nest quite well. The gore-slathered mouths of the nasty buggers were more like little suckholes with sharp teeth.

Temporarily paralyzed in fear, Walt stood there like he'd become a statue, as if even the slightest movement would alert the blind larvae and they would go into attack mode. Then he saw what they were feasting on. Well, he heard it first, the soft moaning of agony. Bodies, unmoving but alive, breathing shallow, strained, wet breaths. Jaundiced eyes, red and wet with a constant trickle of tears. One was missing arms, in place of which were blood-stumps of gnawed flesh. Another was in a similar predicament with her legs, chewed to nubs below her knees. Somehow they were still conscious, suffering through the slow torture of being eaten alive by mutated wasp larvae.

Gunshots from the cave outside of the mud-nest snapped Walt out of his horror-induced trance. At that very moment he saw a familiar face in the breathing food of the larvae, and then the cell phone screen went black.

He fumbled with the phone to get the screen on. The image he was left with floated in his mind like a terrible after-image. He didn't want to see it, but had to be sure.

For his sake and for the sake of Big Vic.

With the cell phone back on, the light created shadows out of the feasting larvae, and one of them was on the ground slurping on a body that must have been dead. The larvae was a particularly boisterous one that made sickening grunts with each mouthful of succulent innards it pulled free from the tear in Brandy's gut.

Walt trembled and then that turned into full-blown shakes. Her face was pale and blemished only with a few scrapes and cuts, bruises that were so dark purple they were black. It was Brandy.

There was no time for Walt to pay his respects or do anything decent for the dead, so he took a picture. The flash caused the larvae to shrink away from Walt, but did little to stop their ravenous hunger.

That was it. Walt got what he came in the cave to get. He had hoped for better results, but at least he could put Big Vic's mind to rest. It would be little consolation and he was sure Vic would now hold him responsible for her death. In some twisted way he held himself responsible for Brandy's death. If only . . .

The larvae were becoming acutely aware of Walt's presence, some of them removing their mouths from suckling bloody nubs to sniff the fresh fruit. Walt pulled his gun and pointed it at the larvae, but what use would it be for him to shoot them? The bullets might ricochet and end up giving him a good sting.

Worried that he would become a fresh feast for the perpetually hungry, Walt decided to take his chances in the cave and see what the gunfire was all about. He emerged into slightly less darkness with his gun drawn, prepared to let off a round were a wasp to close in on him. He wasn't a good shot. Mostly carried the guns for protection since he dealt in such large quantities of methamphetamines. He'd never had to shoot at anyone, but he'd pulled his piece to illustrate a threat. When push comes to shove he didn't know if he had it in him to pull the trigger on a fellow doper, but he figured it wouldn't be hard to plug one of these wasps.

Outside of the mud nest Walt took a moment to look around and re-familiarize himself with the contours of the cave. The wasps were flying in circles and seemingly random zigzags, but appeared to have dropped the defensive attitude that had caused Walt to run for cover. To his right was the body pile. Food for the maggoty birthlings.

Walt's nerves were jangled from both the excitement within the cave and the need for drugs. He had always dealt with sticky situations by smoking some meth. It was a cure-all. At least that's what Walt told himself. A lot of his shattered nerves were a result of addiction, something he was all too aware of, something that gnawed at his mind like those wasp larvae gnawed on arm stumps. Whereas once he got high for leisure and fun, he now used out of necessity and addiction.

The body pile was close to the wall of the cave, so Walt decided to go in that direction. It seemed like a suicide mission to cavort right through the middle of the place below the frenzied wasps. They'd skewer Walt like a living shish kabob.

The closer he came to the haphazard pile of human bodies, the worse the smell became. Nikki had told him that some of them had died and were rotting, which was clear, but also that their bowels and bladders had released. It was like an unkempt restroom in the middle of an unkempt slaughterhouse. Up close the odor was horrendous. As it turned out, that was something to take Walt's mind off of the tickle in his brain that yearned for dope.

Slowly making his way around the back of the bodies, doing everything not to look at them, Walt was startled by a movement. He just about yelped, but clamped a hand over his mouth. He bit into two fingers hard enough to draw blood, but he didn't notice. It took a moment for him to realize that he was looking at the girl he and Matt met in the cave. Her eyes were wide white orbs of surprise in a dirty face.

Nikki said, "You're okay."

Walt nodded. "Where's Matt?"

She shook her head and swallowed hard. "Over there somewhere. I heard the gunshots. I hope they didn't get him." She licked her lips and gritted sand in her teeth. "I saw where you came from."

Walt's eyes were darting around, as they so often did. "Back there? Yeah." He started shaking his head like someone who was one outburst away from a mental hospital.

"I saw it too. That's what I was telling you and Matt about. Those are the larvae. But they got human faces. Kind of. I couldn't imagine what kind of mess they would make if they breastfed."

Walt wrinkled his brow. "The fuck?"

Nikki shook her head. "Nothing. I think of crazy shit sometimes. But really, those weird mouths would take a nipple off."

Walt's face scrunched up at the comment. "Lets head to the front of the cave. I think that's where Matt is. I found what I came in here to find, and you guys don't have any friends left in here, right?"

Nikki nodded. "Right."

"Then let's get the fuck out of here."

They stuck to the shadows following the same path Nikki had tread with Shawna in tow. Their heads were on swivels, constantly checking the wasps. The wasps' agitation was lessening, but the threat was real. As Nikki and Walt neared the first of two cave openings, they saw Matt's outline in the darkness.

"Where the hell have you two been?" Matt said. He was crouched down with the contents of his backpack neatly arranged on the cave floor: a Coleman propane canister, a couple of lighters, a can of lighter fluid, his gun, extra rounds, a roll of duct tape, two bottles of water, and a rather large ring of keys.

Nikki dropped to the floor of the cave and lurched for one of the bottles of water. "Good god I'm thirsty!"

"Not too much," Matt said. "Those are the only two bottles we have."

Walt licked his lips. "You sure you didn't already drink one? Them two are full."

"Yeah, I had some water."

"Way I see it one of them is mine and one is hers." Walt reached for the second bottle of water, but Matt grabbed it first. Walt scowled. "What gives?"

Nikki capped her bottle. "Watch your voice."

"He needs to share the goddamned water. He's already drank one. That's not fucking fair."

Matt glared up at Walt from his crouched position. "Look, I know where a whole ice chest of water is. We brought a bunch with us. We can get it once we get out of here."

Walt nervously checked on the wasps. His mouth was drier than ever now that water was in sight. "Well give me a drink, dammit. Don't hold out. That's fucked up."

Nikki handed over the bottle she had drank from. "Here."

Walt hesitated a moment, eyes trained on the fresh bottle of water in Matt's hand. He grabbed Nikki's bottle and took a generous drink, keeping his thoughts to himself.

"So I have a plan," Matt said. "You got all that damn dope in your backpack, Walt. You still got it, right?" Matt cocked a snaky grin.

"Fuck off, man. I haven't even opened up the backpack."

"Good. We're going to smoke 'em out."

Nikki's face scrunched. "What?"

Matt glanced at her and then returned his attention to Walt. "What's in the backpack, a couple three, four pounds of meth? We packed it with dry brush 'n' shit. We just have to get the backpack in the middle of the cave, douse it in lighter fluid, and let her rip. The meth will ignite and smolder. Way I see it, it should release clouds of noxious smoke.

Bees and wasps 'n' shit don't like smoke, and this smoke will kill them, no doubt. Only problem are these cave openings."

Nikki nodded. "Too drafty."

"Yeah, might be. Don't really know what to expect, but creating as much of a vacuum as possible isn't a bad idea. If we could somehow collapse one of these openings."

Walt scratched his cheeks incessantly, a tick that was a result of oncoming dope-sickness. He swallowed over and over, suffering from terrible cottonmouth. While Matt was speaking, he had finished the bottle of water and was now eyeing the one in Matt's hand.

Nikki reached over the contents of Matt's backpack and grabbed the small propane canister. She looked at it and nodded. "This could do some damage." Nikki eyed the arch of the cave's opening. "We don't have to get too high up. Maybe we could cram this canister between some of those rocks. Hit it with a bullet." She made a sound like an explosion, but soft enough not to arouse the wasp's attention.

Matt bit his lower lip, eyes squinted in thought, head raised just enough to spy on the wasps lingering at the ceiling of the cave, and then he smiled. "Goddamn, girl, I like the way you think."

The tunnels throughout the mountain had been smoothed with some kind of mud, however the cave itself, for the most part, was just like any other cave, with rocks and boulders jutting from the walls, particularly around the arches of the two entry points, both of which were about six to eight feet tall.

After a moment studying the shorter of the two openings, Nikki said, "I'm the smallest." She looked Walt from head to toes, only now noticing the sad shape of the man, the sunken face and gangly frame. "Well, I think I am. The rocks look sturdy. I could climb up and fit the canister somewhere close to the top."

Matt grabbed his gun and checked the ammunition, filling it with spare rounds. "I'll cover you, Walt."

Walt reared his head back. "What?"

Matt handed Walt the lighter fluid and a lighter. "You got the backpack with the meth. Crawl out to the middle of the cave and douse it in lighter fluid. Light that son of a bitch. As soon as you have it lit, I'll shoot the canister like at the end of Jaws, blow the goddamned opening to rubble. Then we'll have to make tracks to the other opening before we all have an overdose on that smoke."

"I'm not going out there," Walt protested.

Matt's eyes deepened. "C'mon, man, we all have a job to do. That's how we're going to get out of here."

"Why don't we just get out of here? Why do we have to act out some stupid plan?"

Nikki sighed. "We're all in danger in here. If we just leave, we're still in danger. Smoking them out may or may not work, but have you been keeping an eye on them? Huh? Have a look."

Both Walt and Matt pivoted their heads upward. The wasps were clustered together at the apex of the cave's ceiling, lined up like a winged army, their dead eyes all staring at the humans attempting to disrupt their mountain sanctuary.

Nikki said, "I have a feeling that if we're hasty they'll be on us. I think we're going to have to move fast, but cautiously." She looked directly into Walt's bloodshot eyes. "You have to trust that Matt will cover you."

Walt shook his head. "This is crazy." They were all sweating, but Walt was absolutely pouring. He looked horrible like a man pulled from a sickbed.

Nikki nodded in agreement. "Yes, it is." And then she got up, walked to the mouth of the cave and began her delicate one-armed climb of the rock.

Matt cocked a bullet into the chamber and said, "It's show

time. Get out there, and be quick. Light it and run. I got your back. Believe me."

Walt made a deflated sort of sound, shrugged, and crawled across the cave floor with about as much grace as a malformed giraffe. His hair hung in dripping, sweaty strands that stung his eyes, but he was focused and determined and beginning to feel dopesick. If he could use that to his advantage, as a sort of dangling carrot . . . Was the carrot more dope, a quick nose full once they got out of the cave, or was it a second chance? Burn the dope and start over?

Several of the wasps unlatched themselves from the ceiling, dive bombing for Walt as he scampered towards the center of the cave. Matt took aim and pulled off a couple of rounds, missing the wasps, but startling them enough to go into a frenzied flight pattern that bought Walt some time. Matt yelled, "Just light the bag and high tail it!"

Matt let off another shot and hit a wasp in the abdomen. It went down fast, rolling on the cave floor and shedding bloody arms and hands until it came to a stop. "I don't have a lot of ammo!"

Nikki found a viable crook in the rocks and placed the propane canister upright to create a good target. She then climbed the few feet back down and joined Matt. "It's ready, but I've seen you shoot. Give me the gun."

This caught Matt off guard. "What? I'm not giving you the gun."

"You said you're running out of bullets. Give me the gun. I can hit it."

Matt's machismo got the better of him. He shook his head. "No, I don't think so." He hollered to Walt, "You lighting that thing? C'mon!"

"Seriously," Nikki said, "I used to target practice with my dad. I can hit the target no problem." This time she reached for the gun, but Matt pulled it back.

"Hey, watch it!" His eyes went into a V of anger, something that was intimidating to even the toughest guys, but Nikki wasn't having any of it.

Nikki became enraged. "Goddammit, Matt, cut it out. If you want to get out of here give me the goddamned gun. You're gonna waste the remaining bullets chipping away at rock. I. Can hit. The target."

Matt stared at Nikki like he was looking into the face of a crazy woman, as if her demands were unwarranted and absurd. As if a woman had no right to use a gun. Matt considered himself a lover of women, but he harbored many a misogynist viewpoint. He would sooner allow Nikki to make him a sandwich than allow her to use the gun. And yet he hesitated. The smartass remark that would normally eject itself from his uncouth maw was stuck in his throat. It was the look in Nikki's eyes. There was a burning, and intensity that was a convincing ploy or some kind of truth that she had experience with guns that Matt lacked. Because Matt was a shit aim and he knew it. *Maybe she really did shoot targets with her dad.*

Nikki reached out her hand, but was wary of grabbing the gun. It would be up to Matt to hand it over.

Walt hollered, "What the fuck is going on over there?" He opened up the bag, tempted to scrape off a chunk of the meth, something he could put in his pocket for later when they got out of this damn cave, but decided against it. If he got out of this, he promised himself that he was done with drugs. He'd enter rehab or a halfway house or something. He would need help, and a lot of it. Drugs and alcohol would be an easy way to get the sight of those things feasting on Brandy out of his mind. He doused the meth, dry brush, and backpack with the entire can of lighter fluid. He then took one of the lighters and used his fingernails to pull on the little copper mechanism where the fluid seeped out and would create a flame from a spark flicked off of the roller. Pulling that little copper piece out created a steady stream of butane that, once Walt rolled the spark, would create a flame that would not go out without blowing on it. He used to do this for fun to watch lighters blow up once the flame traveled into the little reservoir containing the butane. He then tossed that into the backpack and the lighter fluid ignited. It was a gentle ignition, unlike gasoline, which would have been preferable, but the bag was lit and Walt was on his feet, running as if his life depended on it. And it did.

Walt pulled the gun from his waistband. He was mildly surprised that it hadn't fallen out. Holding a gun in a waistband like people did in movies always seemed, to him, like such bullshit. He slowed as he met up with Nikki and Matt, who were in some kind of standoff.

Walt looked at both of them, studying their faces, and then scanned the cave for potential danger. Wisps of smoke rose from the backpack, but seeing it from this distance put things into ugly perspective. Would a couple pounds of smoldering meth do anything at all? Suddenly, like some force of nature, Walt regretted everything. He wished that he had all that meth. He could just run off and leave Nikki and Matt to their silent bickering. He could find a good spot out in the desert and snort speed until his nose bled.

Walt closed his eyes tight and shook his head to snap out of it. "What are you guys doing? Let's get out of here. The bag is on fire, man!"

Nikki inched her hand out just a bit more, hoping that would be enough for Matt to drop his inhibitions and hand over the gun. Holding her stare into Matt's eyes, she said, "Walt, how many bullets you have left? Do you know?"

Walt licked his lips, swallowed hard. "Not sure. A few at least."

"How good a shot are you?"

"Not good at all. I have the guns for intimidation, man. I've never used them."

She smirked. "Of course you haven't. Since Matt here can't

drop the macho bullshit so we can get the fuck out of here, maybe you could let me use that there pistol to hit the propane canister. What do you think? You ready to get the fuck out of here?"

Walt nodded, head darting around for sneaky wasps. "Fuck yeah I'm ready."

Matt gritted his teeth tight, breathing heavily though his nose. The gun trembled in his hand.

Still staring into Matt's squinted eyes but talking to Walt, she said, "Then hand it over."

Walt moved to hand her his pistol, but Matt placed his gun into Nikki's waiting hand. "Fuck it. Show us what you got."

Matt backed up in the direction of the other cave entrance where they would all exit together. He didn't take his eyes off of Nikki.

Nikki grabbed the gun with both hands the way her father taught her. She squinted one eye and got the target in her sights. The little forest green canister was more difficult to see in the dark than she expected. She could feel Matt's eyes on her but knew better than to allow him to cause her nerves to kick in. Nikki took in a deep breath and let it out while loosening her joints, and then pulled the trigger.

At the very moment the canister exploded, a flash of movement caught Matt's eyes. He yelled for Walt's attention, but the sound of the canister, followed immediately by the cave's mouth breaking apart and crumbling in a rain of rock and small boulders, was too loud for him to be heard. In that moment a wasp broke from the pack zipping around the ceiling and zeroed in on Walt. Matt stumbled backwards, startled by the ace shot that blew the canister, and also by the girth of the wasp at such close proximity. It grabbed Walt with its many hands and jerked upward, but the sound of rock crumbling and the subsequent dirt that lifted into a cloud that met the menial smoke rising from the backpack threw the wasp into a barrel roll.

The crumbling of the cave opening loosened rocks above the second opening, dropping a large boulder that, for an instant, took Nikki's breath away. In that moment she could see their only chance of escape being taken away, but alas the one boulder only partially concealed the opening, creating even more of a vacuum for the smoldering dope, and leaving enough room for their getaway.

Nikki retreated from the crumbling mouth of the cave where she had shot the propane canister and instinctually headed for the second opening where they were to make their big getaway. She was only vaguely aware that something bad had happened. She passed by Matt, but hesitated at the edge of the other opening. She turned and followed Matt's gaze just in time to see the wasp spinning toward the wall of the cave, but in the last moment it caught its bearings and pulled out of the barrel roll like a stunt jet in an air show.

Matt's face was blank. "It fucking got Walt!"

As the wasp drew Walt high into the cave to mingle with its brethren, Walt's gun fell and clattered on the cave floor. Matt made a gesture to retrieve it, but checked himself. Too much risk. If one wasp found the bravery to capture Walt the others were no doubt considering the same move to get Nikki and Matt.

The dust cloud caused Matt to choke and cough. He covered his mouth with his arm and made his way toward Nikki. "Can you get a shot on the one with Walt?"

Nikki shook her head. "Too risky. Besides, if it dropped Walt he'd die from the fall."

"What do we do?"

"I don't know."

The area of the cave that they collapsed had small opening openings where starlight illuminated swirling dust, but none large enough for a wasp to pass through. The idea that they created a vacuum was ridiculous and laughable. They should have run.

Matt palmed his face. "We can't leave him."

"I know."

"What do we do?"

As they watched a small army of massive wasp-things hovering around and clinging to the ceiling of a cave in the middle of the Mojave Desert, there was a distinct change in the smoke that rose from the remains of the backpack at the center of the cave. What had started as wisps of black smoke had become thick, white plumes. It was impossible to tell whether it had anything to do with collapsing the second cave opening, but the desert winds became stronger, swirling the thick smoke that rose to the ceiling, further irritating the wasps.

"The smoke is getting thicker," Nikki said. "They're gonna have to go somewhere. Either through the mouth of the cave or the tunnels. I'm thinking they're going to seek out fresh air. Let's step outside and watch. The one with Walt is bound to come this way."

"So, what, you're going to try and shoot it then?"

Nikki nodded. "That's our only chance. That's Walt's only chance."

Matt shrugged. "Well shit, you proved you're a good shot, and I want to get the fuck out of here. Let's do it."

As the meth-tainted smoke lifted to the ceiling of the cave, Nikki and Matt stepped through the rock arch and into the warm desert air of early morning. With the moon on the other side of the mountain, the stars were brilliant and limitless. Millions of them twinkling, constellations that stood out like images from a textbook. After spending so much time inside the cave this magnificent view of the universe was truly awe-striking, but there was no time to admire nature.

Matt crouched on one side of the cave and Nikki on the other. Now that they were outside it was difficult to see through the darkness of the cave. The collective buzzing became more frantic.

Matt wiped sweat off his face. "They're going to zip out of there at high speeds. We have to stay back. If one of them bumps into us it'll knock us down the mountain. Probably kill us."

Nikki nodded, but didn't say anything. Her eyes were trained on the cave. She couldn't see anything but the thickening smoke.

Matt said, "You really think you will be able to hit the wasp when it shoots out of there?"

Her eyes never left the cave. "Clay pigeons are my specialty."

"Yeah, but can you hit the wasp and not Walt?"

"I hope. If I don't try he's going to die anyway."

"This is crazy. Maybe we should just go. C'mon, we're outside now. We made it out! I don't even know Walt. He's some fucking junkie. Did you know that?"

Nikki wrinkled her brow, only now averting her deft attention from the inside of the cave. "Really? You would just leave him in there?"

"I don't know the guy from a hole in the ground. He's a drug dealer. I don't have sympathy for fucking drug dealers."

"Look, I don't know what the guy does for a living and I don't care. I couldn't live with myself if I didn't at least try to save him. You don't have to stay." She removed her glare from Matt and focused on the cave again. "I don't need you. No, I have an idea. Why don't you try and get a call out to the police. You got bars?"

Matt pulled his phone. "One bar. I could probably get a call out now."

"Why don't you shine the light into the cave so I can see what we're dealing with."

Matt did as she asked. The light did little to illuminate the cave, but that was mostly due to the fact that the cave was thick with smoke. Matt grinned. "Holy shit, it's working."

A sound like something heavy hitting the floor of the cave issued, causing a ripple in the wafting smoke.

Nikki crouched and adjusted the sweaty grip on her gun. "I hope that wasn't Walt falling."

There was another sound similar to the first, and this time Nikki could see the form. An arm jettisoned from the felled wasp landing close to the mouth of the cave.

"They're dropping," Matt said. "Fuckin'-A, they're dying aren't they?"

"The rest are going to come this way. Any minute now. Watch yourself."

And they did just that. One after the other they emerged from the smoke toward the mouth of the cave at high speed. Some of them were disoriented enough to misjudge their departure, which caused them to slam into the side of the cave or clip the edge of the fallen boulder. Either way, these miscalculations were met with severe injury or death on impact. The ones that hit the edges were flung outside of the cave, tossed down the mountain and battered by jutting rocks. Matt had to thrust himself backward to avoid being entangled in a wasp that careened into the edge of the cave and went into an awkward roll. He felt the air rush by him as the failed creature went flying and he almost lost his balance and had his own tumble.

Nikki continued watching as they emerged, one eye squinted, the other with the sights lined up. She shot clay pigeons with a rifle, which had a scope for accuracy. Lining up two sights on a moving target was going to be damn near impossible. Her focus would have to be on hitting the wasp in a large area, such as the abdomen, to give her some slop. Hopefully Walt didn't become collateral damage. Hopefully she could—

Several wasps had successfully launched themselves from

the cave into the fresh desert air, wings buzzing as they did so, and then one approached that was making an entirely different sound, something layered atop the buzzing.

"That's him!" Nikki yelled, but there was no telling if Matt heard her over the wasps' din. She gripped the gun tighter, preparing for the shot. Just one shot. If she didn't hit the wasp with the initial shot it would get too high in the air. Walt wouldn't make the fall.

The screaming intensified quickly, impossible to judge, and then the wasp shot out of the smoky cloud, lined up perfectly for managing the mouth of the cave without a disastrous collision.

Nikki followed the wasp as it was birthed into the night. There was no time to see if Walt was in its clutches. Nikki depended on the scream, the wretched, panicked yell that ripped out of his lungs. Nikki struggled to keep her aim ahead of the beast. Having no experience shooting a moving target at such close proximity, she wasn't sure how far ahead of the target she had to be, if at all. With no time to think about the shot or the target, Nikki pulled the trigger. The blast, not quite as deafening outside of the cave, echoed off of the surrounding mountains. Due to the velocity the wasp gained in its frenzy to escape the toxic smoke, it traveled a good distance even after having its abdomen blown open.

Nikki's mouth dropped, her eyes swelled. The wasp went down in an oblong spin, its wings desperately attempting to right the beast, but unable to. It looped in rapid circles as it drifted to the canyon floor. When it finally hit, it buzzed around in wild circular patterns kicking up clouds of dust that swirled in the wind. The fall was softened by the fluttering wings, but the dying wasp continued to roll across the desert floor, rising into the air a few times in a futile attempt to become airborne, only to collide with the dry earth and spin in random directions, pinging off of stray boulders and cacti until the monstrous insect hit its head hard enough to lose consciousness.

Clouds of sand swirled like miniature tornados, creating a dust bank that obscured any view of Walt.

Another wasp launched from the cave, startling both Matt and Nikki who were focused on the canyon floor, half expecting to see Walt's body lying there shredded from the final actions of the dying mutated wasp. Or maybe he would be standing triumphantly with his arms in the air.

They couldn't tell. Wherever he was, Walt wasn't jumping for joy.

Nikki and Matt began the slow, steady descent of the mountain.

CHAPTER 24

THE MOUTH OF THE CAVE LOOKED LIKE A DARK PATCH OF nothing from the canyon floor. No smoke drifted out and the wasps had either all fled or died. On their search for Walt (hopefully a breathing man and not a body), they came across a whole wasp that had landed and rolled onto its back. The strange humanoid arms twitched and moved slowly with the last vestiges of the beast's nerves. Its head was tilted, the black eyes staring glossily into nothing.

As Nikki and Matt passed that particular wasp, Nikki wondered about the ones that seemed to get away. Just how far would they get? Did they inhale enough toxic smoke to die somewhere off in the desert?

They hollered for Walt, and at first heard nothing. Then there was a sound like someone dying that came from a cluster of rocks.

"Oh shit!" Nikki bolted into a run.

At the base of the mountain Nikki called for Walt. She was unsure how he would have become caught in this cluster of rocks, considering the winding and jerky path the dying wasp had taken. It hadn't gone very close to the area where the voice came from, however Nikki rationalized that with all of the dust and the time it took for her and Matt to climb down the mountain, Walt might have crawled to the rock cluster where he felt safe.

A hand emerged from a small opening in the rocks.

Nikki dropped to her knees before the hand. "Walt!" She didn't know this man, had only met him in a dangerous situation, but she felt a sort of responsibility to get him to safety. She and Matt didn't go through crumbling part of a cave and lighting a bag of methamphetamine on fire for nothing. They hadn't risked their lives in a cave full of huge menacing wasps for nothing. Nikki grabbed the hand and pulled, but the guy who emerged from the cluster was not Walt. Nikki's brow wrinkled. "Sammy?"

Matt, who was closer to the wreckage of the wasp Nikki shot out of the sky, turned at the sound of his best friend's name. "What did you say?"

Sammy was glistened like a hog on a spit. His clothes were so wet it looked like he had just stepped out of a pool. He made agonized sounds as if unable to articulate proper words. Nikki helped him to his feet, but his legs were like stalks of old celery. He was too heavy for Nikki to support. Matt saw this and rushed to assist.

Matt put an arm around Sammy's shoulder for support. "Dude, I thought you were a goner." Matt blinked his eyes rapidly to fend off the tears that threatened to breach his lids. Matt had been through a lot in the past twenty-four hours and couldn't keep the tears from flowing.

Sammy, seeing this rare show of emotion, did his best to grin and said, in a gravelly voice: "Pussy."

Matt could have punched him in the shoulder like he used to when they were in junior high school, but the comment put a twinkle in his eye and he sobbed out a laugh.

"You got him?" Nikki asked.

Matt nodded and Nikki moved on in search of Walt. The wasp was curled into a ball, its abdomen torn open with thick clouds of stomach and intestine like wet stuffing from a torn couch. Arms were missing, the face was scraped and torn severely, right down to something that was a blend of skull and exoskeleton. Walt was nowhere in sight. Nikki circled the dead wasps, and that's when she saw trails in the sand as if something had been dragged or dragged itself. She didn't have to follow the trail for too long before she found Walt.

He collapsed twenty yards from the offending wasp. His clothes were torn and dusty with desert sand. The exposed parts of his body were so torn from the abuse he sustained while the wasps struggled with flight in its dying moments that he was caked with sand. Some patches were dark with blood that looked like fresh gardening soil. A laceration across his face was so bad that Nikki could see what she thought were his molars, red, wet and gleaming under starlight.

Nikki knelt beside Walt and shook him gently. "Walt." Another gentle shake. "Walt."

He moved slowly at first, and then snapped his head toward her, one eye open wide and the other pinned shut by red swollen flesh.

"Are you shot? I got the wasp, but did the bullet get you too?"

He shook his head slowly. "I . . . I don't think so."

It was a strange feeling that swept over Nikki. A swell of pride. There was no way of knowing that they had exterminated all of the giant wasp-things, no way of knowing that the larvae hadn't survived and were currently feasting on dying humans trapped in a mud nest in some suspended state of near-death. She knew one thing. She had saved a man's life.

Nikki smiled, which turned out to be infectious, for,

despite his lacerated cheek, Walt met her smile with a weak version all his own. Nikki said, "My dad told me I was a regular Annie Oakley. I guess he was right. How are your legs? You think you can stand?"

Walt shifted, gritting his teeth and groaning. "I think I can stand, with some help. Must have broken some ribs. Maybe my arm. Fuckin' body hurts all over."

Nikki stood and held her arms out. "Here, I'll help you. We're still out in the middle of the desert, and I'd like to try and get back to the road before sunrise."

Walt stood with Nikki's assistance, grimacing and sucking air through his teeth as fresh pains assaulted his body. He shook his head. "Goddamn, man. I thought shock was supposed to do something about the pain."

"We're almost out of this. You've just got to push through it, that's all. Look at what you've overcome. You were wasp food for sure. It's amazing you're alive."

Walt chuckled. It was a sad sound considering the phlegm in his throat and the state of his cheek. "Wasp food. Who'd a thunk it?"

Matt and Sammy shuffled across the dry desert floor, Sammy gaining his footing with each step. "Holy shit!" Matt said. "I thought you were dead for sure, dude!"

"I *feel* dead."

Matt clamped a hand on Walt's shoulder the way he would a good friend he hadn't seen in a while. Walt grimaced and ducked away from Matt's domineering grip. Matt said, "Shit, dude. Sorry." Matt looked him up and down. "You really got fucked up."

Walt closed his mouth and shuffled his tongue around his gums and inner cheeks. He spit out a tooth and said, "Let's get the fuck out of here. Big Vic's waiting and I've got some bad news for him."

The four slowly strode through the slender crevice that led

them out of the mountains. They walked in silence, all reflecting on what they had been through. It was unbelievable, surreal. Fighting off giant mutated wasps was the kind of thing that turned into legendary stories, but who would even believe such a story? Would there be a cover up or would this make the news?

As the group approached Big Vic, who sat propped against a rock, they could see the hope in his eyes flee. His daughter wasn't among the survivors.

Walt broke from the pack. "We did everything we could."

Vic looked him up and down. "You look like hell."

A strained laugh came out of Walt's mouth. "You don't even known, pops."

"I sat here and thought about it. Had a long time to think. It was stupid coming out here." He shook his head. "What was I thinking? I—"

Walt cut Big Vic off. "No, you were right."

Vic reared his head back in confusion. "I don't—" and then he understood.

Walt pulled out his phone. "I saw her, but . . ."

Vic slumped. "Aw shit."

"I knew you wouldn't believe me, so I took a picture." Walt reached his hand out with the phone, but Vic put one hand out and turned away.

"I don't need to see that." After a moment of whipping winds and swirling sand, Big Vic said, "I believe you." A tear made a trail through the dust on his face and dripped onto his shirt.

Though genuinely touched, Walt turned his phone off and decided that he would save the photo if ever Big Vic needed proof. He would never look at the picture, but it would be there if closure was needed.

Through the wind a new sound rose, one that had everyone on edge. It was a buzzing sound.

"Oh shit," Nikki said. "I hope we didn't piss of a whole battalion of those things."

Matt perked up, listening closely. He shook his head. "No. Not wasps. Help."

In the distance a dune buggy with a trail of sand in its wake plowed forward. The desert machine came to a stop. Shifting winds blew the sand over the dune buggy like a wave of fog. When it cleared they could see Ollie in the passenger seat and a man with flowing gray hair and a red bandana over his face at the wheel.

The driver pulled his bandana down and whooped. "You guys need a lift!"

For the third time Matt said, "Damn, Ollie, I thought you were a goner for sure."

Ollie shook his head. "I've brought the cavalry."

It was a six-seater dune buggy with an engine so gleaming with chrome it looked brand new. The driver got out, but left the engine running. "There's five seats, but we can make due. Let's get you out of here. My wife and some friends are waiting back at the highway in the motorhome. Ollie here flagged us down, and he was damn lucky. Ain't no one on the highway at four in the morning. That's the way we like it. Travel when everyone else is sleeping. We put a call in to the police."

The driver helped get Big Vic into the buggy and then the rest of the survivors climbed in. Nikki, being the smallest and less injured of the group, positioned herself between two seats rather than sit on someone's lap. She held tight to the roll cage above them and the buggy took off. They made it back to the motorhome and waited for the authorities. Nikki separated herself from the group and gazed upon the mountain, wondering about the possibilities. What exactly would the authorities do, if anything at all? There were carcasses of dead wasps that could be examined. Would they even bother investigating the labyrinthine tunnel system? The cave?

Did any of the wasps get away?
What other secrets did the desert hide?

The End

ACKNOWLEDGMENTS

Thank you to Paul Goblirsch at Thunderstorm Books for believing in this book enough to publish it in a signed/limited edition. Thank you to David Sodergren, Alicia Stamps, John Bender, and Danielle Kaheaku for reading an early draft of the book and offering your wonderful insights. Thank you to Danny Richardson for being a major supporter of my work, and for his help getting the right eyes on this book in the first place. Big thanks to Sean Duregger and Encyclopocalypse Publications not only for finally getting this book a trade release, but working tirelessly getting this book ready for public consumption. Thank you to my family for their support. And a huge thank you to my dad for the offhand comment that planted the seed in my mind: "That would make for a great science fiction novel." Naturally, I used the idea in a horror novel.

About the Author

Robert Essig is the author of more than fifteen books such as Circus Oasis, Mojave Mud Caves, Tweaker Creatures, and Follow the Maggot Wagon. He has published over 150 short stories and edited three small press anthologies including Chew On This! (Blood Bound Books), which was nominated for a Splatterpunk Award. Robert lives with his family in east Tennessee.

Also by Robert Essig

Through the In Between, Hell Awaits

People of the Ethereal Realm

In Black

Death Obsessed

Ain't Worth a Shit (with Jack Bantry)

Insatiable (with Jack Bantry)

Stronger Than Hate

Shallow Graves (with Jack Bantry)

Brothers In Blood

Salpsan

Tweaker Creatures

Follow the Maggot Wagon

The Evil Awakens trilogy:

Terror of Rattlesnake Mountain

Ghost of Rattlesnake Mountain

Cult of Rattlesnake Mountain

The Circus Oasis

Mojave Mud Caves